I0571092

DEVASTATED

The Wastelands Series Book 1

MIA HEINTZELMAN

LeviLynn

Devastated

Copyright © 2020 by Mia Heintzelman

All rights reserved. No part of this book may be reproduced or utilized in any form or by any electronic or mechanical means, now known or hereafter invented, including photocopying and recording, xerography, or in any information storage and retrieval systems, without written permission from the author, except for the use of brief quotations in a book review.

First Levi Lynn Books edition June 2020.

Levi Lynn Books can bring authors to your live event. For more information or to book an event, visit our website at www.miaheintzelman.com.

Editing by Faith Freewoman

Cover design and Formatting by Tangled Covers

Manufactured in the United States of America

Cataloguing-in-Publication Data

ISBN: 978-0-9990493-8-9

Name: Heintzelman, Mia, author.

Title: Devastated / Mia Heintzelman

Description: Mia Heintzelman | Las Vegas: Mia Heintzelman, 2020.

Subjects: Romance | Dark fiction.

This is a work of fiction. Names, characters, places and incidents are either the product of the author's imagination or are used fictitiously, and any resemblance to actual persons, living or dead, business establishments, events or locales is entirely coincidental.

For the roses who grew through concrete.

CHAPTER ONE

IZZY

FOR SOMEONE WHOSE LIFE WAS IN A CONSTANT STATE OF change, I should have been better at adjusting. I should have been able to slap on a smile, slip into my thick skin, and be the new girl for the fifth time without a second thought—at least for Dad's sake.

Except everything about this time felt different.

Usually, like clockwork, every two years it was a new school. With it, another quaint little two-bedroom rental with a rickety, stiff twin bed. And, as always, the sidewinding battle to snag myself space in some town's carefully woven fabric.

But this time Dad was deploying for six months and I was going to be on my own.

"I can hear you narrating in your head..." Dad's bushy brows lifted impossibly high, but he didn't take his eyes off the road. He didn't have to. He knew me better than anyone else on the planet. Ever since I was eight, it's been only us—a decade's worth of Dad knowing what I was thinking without me having to say a word.

"It's really not going to be that bad, Izz. I promise. I've

known Quincy since before you were born. He's a good guy, and it makes me feel better about this whole boarding school thing, knowing you'll have a support system close by."

"...so you keep telling me."

The gravelly road made a sudden sharp curve and Dad overcorrected, sending the car fishtailing and kicking up desert dust. "Shit." He stomped on the brake and pumped the gas like he was in some chase scene in an action movie, except with his arm crowbarred across me until the car finally slowed and straightened out. But as he leaned all the way forward against the steering wheel and squinted into the light, the dust began to settle, and Gale Manor came into view.

"Holy—"

"Watch your mouth. I'm still your father." Dad winked as he eased the car around the circular drive and parked next to the stairs leading up to the door.

My mouth fell wide open as I stared at a monstrosity with pillars, dormers, and far too many windows to be on one side of a home. It was one of those great big, gaping houses. The ones that look more like an ode to Tara from *Gone with the Wind* or *Best Little Whorehouse in Texas*, than an inhabitable place for normal people.

"I thought you said you served in the military with him. This is not some middle-class, two-story house. It's a damn mansion, or...a brothel."

At this, Dad shook his head, laughing, and turned to me. "I'm getting a bit worried about the places your mind goes. What have you done with my sweet, innocent daughter? Because I don't know where you get this stuff. Brothels? Really?"

I left the topic right out there in left field where it belonged and peered down at my dress—yes, dress. Black, knee-length, with cap sleeves, and the only formal article of

2

clothing I owned. The last time I wore it, the hem puddled around my calves.

"He did say 'manor,'" Dad inserted himself, uninvited into my thoughts. "I hoped you would wear something with color. You used to love purple and wear the amethyst ring I got you, but...I guess anything is better than your usual uniform of black pants and a black shirt."

"Dad, we're in the middle of the desert in Nevada and we're visiting someone's plantation. I feel like I should be wearing a fancy Kentucky Derby hat and a frilly dress. What's his son like? Is he a pretty little silver spoon?"

I massaged my temples. I could feel myself shutting down, my heart going haywire as it knocked around in my chest. My leg did this weird, nervous, tic-like bounce. The whole stick-out-like-a-sore-thumb fear crawled up under my skin and settled there.

Of course, this was the moment when light from the house glinted off the car window as the front door flew open and the Stepford Family stood framed in the doorway. Tall, brooding husband. Check. Flawless and fit ladies-who-lunch wife. Check. Fluffy white dog. Check. Disarmingly hot, fuckboy son. Check.

Holy check.

The perfect little platinum blond family living in the perfect manor.

Awesome. If everyone at Desert Badlands Academy looks like them, my brown skin might as well be a flashing beacon, even in my uniform.

Dad hopped out of the car first and practically broke a sweat getting to his friend, while my hand was still clutched around the car door handle.

"Come on Izzy, let's go," he called.

A full ten-second mental countdown later, and I finally cracked the door, stood, and walked the few feet to the steps where Mrs. Fitness America greeted me first. She grabbed me into a tight hug with her wiry arms cinched around me. Light bounced off her glossy, bone-straight mane, sheared just below her slender shoulder blades. Her warm blue eyes peered into me.

"Oh, Derek, she's beautiful. I can't believe how much she's grown up," she purred, and I halfway expected her to pinch my cheeks or wiggle my chin. "Eighteen already. Do you remember me, honey? I'm Evelyn Gale."

I gave a cursory smile but managed to keep my mouth shut. Dad was doing enough talking for both of us.

"Yep," he sighed. "This is her final year. She's all set to start at Colorado State in the fall. If all goes well at Desert Badlands and she's set for the Equestrian program there."

While Dad continued giving them the lowdown on my life plans, I scrutinized the Gales. Everything about them oozed luxury and entitlement. It was in the way they held themselves with an air of effortlessness, like they never worried about anything—never needed to. Their clothes were crisp, but polished and easily spotted for their quality and the lavish lifestyle they intimated.

They were put-together, well-kept people, from their defined bone structure and shimmery hair to their alabaster skin tone and lithe frames. Porcelain dolls. Loaded, filthy rich, porcelain dolls to be careful with.

Just for a moment, I wondered if they would be careful with me.

Once Dad temporarily reached his cap on bragging about me, I got handed off to Quincy Gale, Desert Storm comrade and knower of no spatial boundaries. He hugged me way too hard and too long, and I was completely surprised when he did lift my chin.

"And look at these eyes," he said. "You've got a heart-

4

breaker on your hands, Derek. We'll definitely have to keep an eye on her."

I forced a smile and backed away.

Only I almost tripped and the son was right behind me, and for a split second he held me from behind to steady me. I could feel the warmth of his deft hands blaze over my arms as heat seared through me before he turned me to face him.

Yes, please.

My heart plummeted into my stomach and I swallowed. I could feel heat wash over my cheeks as I looked up into his summery blue-green eyes. He *was* a pretty little silver spoon. And a fuckboy. Albeit a considerably upgraded version, with his shimmery hair neatly tapered around the hairline and side-parted, and that sheen of opulence usually relegated to the billionaire variety.

Oh, and his mouth.

Jesus. His mouth up close did less-than-appropriate things to me. *God, I wish he was a scratch and sniff.*

I peeked up at him, and his eyes darted to my mouth, then back up to my eyes. I did my best to appear unaffected, but my pulse was echoing in my throat.

What am I doing? This move isn't about boys.

And yet my heart didn't seem to get the memo about this guy.

"Oh, I'm sorry." I was both annoyed and embarrassed all at once.

"Don't be."

Good God. Up close, it almost hurt to look directly at him, but I couldn't turn away as he pulled his full bottom lip between his teeth and the corner of his delicious mouth hitched up in a cocky half-grin.

Swoon. *Why are the bad boys always the hottest?*

After a sharp intake of breath, I actually sighed out loud.

He released a low rumble of a chuckle, and I could feel

the deep timbre low in my belly. "I'm Xander, and you must be *the* Izabelle Waters I've heard so much about."

"Izzy." I swallowed. "I mean, all my friends call my Izzy. You can call me Izzy, but if you don't want to, you can call me Izabelle. Whatever you want. I'll answer."

I literally want to die. Why do these words keep coming out of my mouth?

The adorable half-grin spread into a full-blown, sparkly white, full-teeth smile, complete with adorable dimple. The whole thing might as well have been in slow motion for the way his sweeping lashes flapped down.

Holy fuck.

"Why don't we all go inside?" Evelyn suggested. "Dinner is ready in the formal dining room. We're having Cornish hen." She glided into the house and everyone else fell in line, but I was still trying to pick my jaw up off the floor as I closed the door behind me.

The formal dining room suited the exterior of the house with its old money crystal chandelier and Persian rug. That didn't even include the textured walls and expensive china. In the center, a long wooden table spanned the length of the room and seated at least twenty people that I could tell. In front of each chair, she had laid out the most gorgeous and likely priceless dinnerware flanked with full-etiquette silverware.

And now I felt like I was in *Pretty Woman*, because the only thing I could think about was which fork to use so I didn't embarrass Dad in front of his obscenely rich friend.

Quincy sat at the head of the table, stoic and commanding. Dad and Xander reserved the seats flanking Quincy for Evelyn and me, choosing to settle in the two facing seats beside them. I moved to sit next to Dad, but Evelyn placed a gentle hand on my shoulder before I could.

"Why don't you sit next to Xander, honey?" She slid into

the seat between Quincy and Dad. "You two are going to be fast friends, I just know it. He's been at Desert Badlands all four years, and I'm sure he'll introduce you around and help you get settled." She placed her napkin in her lap and peered back up at me through her fringe of thick, fake, black lashes. "Your Dad says you've already moved into your room, so you'll likely become good friends with your room-mate, too."

"Oh, I don't have a roommate," I said. "I figure it's because I'm starting in the middle of the school year, so everyone's probably already doubled up, but it's okay. I kind of like keeping to myself."

My gaze snapped to where Xander scooted his chair closer to mine.

Evelyn's tight smile didn't reach her sharp eyes. I got the distinct feeling she didn't approve, but I couldn't figure why.

"Well now that's a shame," she said. "Xander's eighteenth birthday is coming up. He's a Valentine's Day baby. Anyway, he's having a party. We always rent out the Estrada Suite at the country club for him and his friends, so I'm sure he'll want you there. You'll meet everyone who's anyone, but if you need anything, you just come on out here anytime, or let Xander know, and we'll be glad to help."

"Yes. Anytime," Quincy added before sipping his wine, and I almost missed it, but in my peripheral vision I noticed the edges of Xander's mouth strain. By the way his jaw jutted slightly, I knew his teeth were clenched.

My shoulders tensed and my grip tightened around the patterned sterling silverware.

I nodded my thanks, forked a green bean, and chewed slowly while I considered their family dynamic. Like the finely crafted silver between my fingers, I sensed the beauty and quality of this traditional, heirloom American family was indeed in good condition—original and unaltered, but not without some imperfections. I knew this wasn't the closed-door version.

I mean, what I was seeing was what everyone on social media portrays with their glossy, laughing pictures of the perfectly curated lives they want you to believe they have. But the people who know the other side usually get to see the real stuff. The burnt food, the ceiling leak in the middle of the living room, the post-breakup mashed potatoes and sour cream overeating.

A wave of sadness washed over me, and I didn't know how I was going to deal with the reality of not seeing Dad every day. If there's one thing we've always been with each other, it's real. We've been there, present, whether good or bad, happiness or heartbreak, just us two. And now it was going to feel like a million miles divided us.

When I looked up, Dad was smiling at me because he knew what I was thinking. The whole intuition thing still functioning on all cylinders. I took another bite of hen and shook my head, stifling a grin.

Why can't they just eat chicken like normal people?

"So, tell me, Izzy...do you have any friends or a boyfriend back home?" Quincy asked, which completely irritated me because I felt like the concept of a military brat was lost on him. By the time I even exchanged a phone number or friended someone online, it was time to leave again. And anyways, why did he even care? It wasn't like he was interested in the answer.

I flashed a tight smile. "I have some friends I still keep in touch with. No boyfriend. Never around long enough." I shot Dad a look before rolling my eyes. Hence the whole good-at-keeping-to-myself skill. *Drought still safely intact.*

But then Xander flicked his eyes in the direction of his dad. There was fury in them.

Quincy nodded, yielding to his son. "Ah...that's just as well."

"Do you mind if I excuse myself? I'd like to show Izabelle the grounds." Xander stood out of the blue, hedging his tall frame toward me, which caught me completely off guard, since his tone sounded like he'd have rather murdered me than take me on a tour.

"You've barely touched your food," his mother complained, but it was the throbbing vein in Quincy's forehead that snagged my attention. He looked put out—like Xander personally wronged him—and I felt like we, Dad and me, had somehow landed in the middle of a lion's den.

"I can—" I began, but Xander already took my hand, practically dragging me into the hall.

"What was that about?" I asked as he hustled me toward the dark hallway.

He blew out a flustered breath and raked his long fingers through his amazing hair. He didn't respond immediately, but his easy posture and cocky grin had been replaced by something...darker. A stone façade. His wicked mood apparent.

Then in the next instant his shoulders were pushed back, and his half-lidded gaze was on me. I could feel my eyes go wide and round as I swallowed, not knowing what to expect, but when I parted my lips to venture a question, his mouth crashed down on mine.

It was a hunch, but if this was the welcome I got at an uppity dinner party, maybe Desert Badlands Academy wasn't going to be so bad. This beautiful storm with his delicious mouth on mine might be just what I needed. If nothing else, I sensed it wouldn't be long before my drought was over.

CHAPTER TWO

XANDER

THIS GIRL HAS NO CLUE WHAT SHE'S DOING HERE.

Both my hands were still flat against the wall as I tore my lips away, breathless, heart rapping against my ribs, and studied Izabelle Waters at a whisper's distance. I saw right through her Daddy's little girl routine. So polite and quiet, with her big brown doe eyes and full lips.

Fuck.

Why are they here? She doesn't belong here.

A grunt escaped me, and it was all I could do not to fuck her right there in the hall with our parents in the next room just to prove my point.

"What...did I do something wrong?" she asked. Her eyes fell, her posture sheepish and vulnerable, but she wasn't innocent. I knew girls who were naïve and untainted, and this girl wasn't one of them. Izabelle knew exactly what she was doing with her short black dress and her wild, dark coils all loose and sexy. Innocent girls didn't wear wine-stained red lipstick over a filthy mouth like that. They didn't walk willingly right into my father's snare.

Did I do something wrong?

It's always the same questions. "Did I do something wrong?" "What do you want from me?" "Why are you like this?"

She wasn't fooling anyone. But, as expected, all it took was her appearance in my house to get her caught up in dear old Daddy's crosshairs.

"Don't fucking tell my dad anything about you," I warned Izabelle, and her heavy brows dipped as she shook her head vehemently. Her shoulders tensed and her eyes went wide.

It was more than evident, we both knew she shouldn't be here in this house, or at Badlands for that matter. And Mom, opening her fucking mouth to invite her back here, like she's welcome. And to my party.

Fuck.

Her eyes darted past me down the hall.

Oh, so Daddy doesn't know his sweet little girl isn't so sweet anymore?

A laugh bubbled up inside me. No, she wouldn't tell my father anything.

But Izabelle didn't know the why or think for a second to question the request. What was I going to say? My father is a sick fuck with a fetish for virgins—and he feeds off their innocence?

My eyes immediately fell to her now reddish-pink, swollen lips and the hungry expression on her face.

She wanted me to finish, and who was I not to oblige?

I blinked a few times and nodded as heat seared through me and settled low and deep.

Yeah, let's play this game and see if you ever want to come back.

Izabelle's chest rose and fell, her breasts pressed against me when I slid my left hand down the wall and found her smooth thigh. She gasped, and fuck if it wasn't the hottest thing ever.

"My dad is in the other room," she said, as if it was the

only thing stopping her from being a willing participant. Her fear was adorable. Initially I brought her into the hall to put some space in front of her, get her out of dear ol' Dad's line of sight, but I didn't expect to be affected.

"I saw you watching me." I crawled my fingers beneath her dress. My skin blazed with every inch of her, but when I reached the thin satin fabric of her panties, Izabelle clutched my hand.

She didn't blink. "I'm serious. I can't hurt him."

"Do you want me?" I asked.

"We just met." The way her voice choked, I guessed it was less in response to my question and more like she was trying to convince herself. Her hand was still wrapped tight around my wrist, but her pelvis was pressed firmly against the growing hard-on in my pants.

"But you aren't stopping me, Izabelle." The words came out on a whisper, but in the moment, it was clear she liked the darker side of me. They always did at first.

She sighed, releasing the sexiest little coarse quiver as she glanced down the hall again. She was seemingly still grappling with the truth behind my words when her grip loosened. Before she could say another word, I pried her open and slipped two fingers inside her wet folds. Her breathing hitched and I knew I'd found her spot.

"Xander?" Mom's sinewy voice tore through my haze, pinballing off the walls from the dining room. Izabelle tensed, frozen with fear, but the possibility of getting caught only made it hotter. I stuck another finger inside, feeling her slick, hot flesh.

"Yes, Mother?"

"We're headed into the parlor," she said. "As soon as you're finished showing Izzy around, please join us."

I hummed some noncommittal sound of agreement.

Yeah, I'll get right on that.

I returned my attention to Izabelle. "May I call you Izabelle? I don't much care for the nickname."

She nodded and wrapped her toned legs around me, her back arched fully. The temptation to take her right there against the wall pulsed and throbbed over my skin, but I couldn't yet.

She moaned and bucked around the rhythm of my hand. The darkest part of me didn't give a fuck, but with her father leaving and her late enrollment at Badlands—the fucking wasteland of misfits—there was plenty of time. This was just laying the groundwork—marking my territory.

I covered her mouth with mine to keep her silent, my tongue searching and savoring, but it only slightly muffled the sound.

With every second, my interest in knowing more about this new siren grew.

"Bite your tongue," I instructed, and she obeyed, which only proved to turn me on further. I pushed in deeper and slid the pad of my thumb over her clit, sending a tremble over her.

She was still holding onto me, panting, moaning. I fucking hated how much I loved it. I hiked her dress all the way up until it circled her neck and burrowed my mouth into her black bra. Fuck. She was softer and sweeter than I imagined.

As she shivered and quaked, digging her nails into my back, I held steady.

When she was finished, I slowly lowered her feet to the floor and tasted her on my fingers.

Sweet all the way to her core.

I found myself still watching her as she regained her footing and straightened her panties, bra and dress. How she could still be sheepish and coy when she just came all over my hand, I couldn't fathom.

It wasn't the reaction I expected.

Even the girls who weren't innocent, they beamed with power and plotted their next tryst before the orgasm was over, but not this one. Izabelle Waters recoiled back into her downcast eyes and folded arms.

But then she looked up at me with half-lidded eyes. "Here, let me..." She swiped the pad of her thumb over my lips. "You had a little lipstick."

I watched her for a few seconds longer before finally leading her by her fingertips into my father's parlor. With its mix of dark navy and hunter green hues and wooden surfaces, it was more of a trophy room than a place to smoke cigars and drink brandy. It was his man cave, complete with a taxidermy zoo covering the walls and a formidable, almost haunting fireplace at the helm.

By the way Izabelle gawked, open-mouthed, she seemed intimidated, although at the same time, like she was gathering details for some later use. Likely to refine her judgment of the perfect household my mother worked so hard to pull off.

While she was busy taking it all in, I noticed a small shift in my father's stance. He shot me an icy stare, and by the way his nostrils quivered, and his eyes tightened, I figured my time with Izabelle in the hall was well spent.

"Izzy," her dad's voice echoed off the maple walls as he welcomed her back. The tic at his jaw when he saw our fingertips touching was noteworthy, albeit short-lived. But worth it to see the fire blaze in his eyes.

She won't be your little girl for long.

Immediately, she corrected her oversight by dropping my hand and walking the few feet over to close the distance between them.

Reassurance.

It appeared we weren't the only family putting our best foot forward this evening.

"So...how'd you like the house?" His brows were still braided together as he scrutinized me.

To her credit, Izabelle didn't miss a beat. She flushed and plastered on a winning smile as she shook her head, as if in awe. "Dad...I can't even tell you how amazing this house is. It's even bigger than it looks. The rooms, the bathrooms," she listed, seemingly careful, calculated enough not to give too many details as she turned toward Mom. "You have a beautiful home."

No. Izzy wasn't innocent. Subtle. Careful with others' feelings. But not to be underestimated in the least.

Mom gushed, modestly pressing her hand over her breast. "Oh, I'm so glad. We're really proud of our home."

As expected, Dad moved to Mom's side.

Ah, the united front.

But, like I always did whenever there was prey in the room, I watched his eyes, the way they roamed, scraping the surface, ravenous to get deeper. They crawled the length of Izabelle's willowy body. From her feet to her tight ass, up to her perky breasts and the delicate curve of her still-flushed neck, he was itching for more—jonesing to scratch it.

He glided his tongue over his lips—until he noticed me watching and straightened.

Yes, Father. I see you. I always see you.

My dad was everything I hated about money and sex and power—what they did to a man. Quincy Gale was the reason I went to the darkest lengths not to be like him.

"What I want to know is how much my little girl is going to miss me." Mr. Waters sidled up to Izabelle and put his arm over her shoulder with a squeeze. "Six months is way too long."

She leaned her head on his shoulder for a moment, then smiled up at him. "I know, Dad. Way too long."

"Well, I'm sure you'll enjoy the equine program. They'll be

lucky to have you, Izzy. Quincy was just telling me the stables are world-renowned. Beautiful paddocks, horse barns, tack rooms. There are farriers and veterinarians on staff. The facility sounds amazing." Mr. Waters turned to Dad. "You know Izzy worked a few summers shadowing an equine vet. She loves horses. To tell you the truth, the relationship she has with them is far better than the ones she has with humans."

I opened my mouth to join in the conversation but rethought it and continued listening. The more I learned about Izabelle Waters, the easier it would be to send her back to whatever hole she crawled out of.

My dad said, "We owned a Saddlebred a few years back, but you know what they say. Horses will eat you out of house and home. My board bill looked like a mortgage."

Mr. Waters laughed a deep, guttural laugh, and I rolled my eyes because the pissing contest was getting old. It wasn't even a contest.

They were all the same, my dad's friends. It was always about who you knew and how much you had. Derek Waters knew Quincey Gale, and apparently, even when it was nothing, you still boasted about the shine of the pennies. The best in one-upmanship.

Frankly, the whole night was getting stale and I was about ready to excuse myself, maybe take Izabelle back to the hallway, when I looked over. She was watching me again. There was definitely something intriguing, alluring about her. I raked my fingers through my hair and sniffed them as I met her gaze, only to be met with a sexy smile toying at her lips. And just in case she'd forgotten, I slipped my middle finger in my mouth and sucked.

Oh, it's a shame I have to ruin this one.

CHAPTER THREE

IZZY

MY GOALS WERE SIMPLE: BLEND IN, GET SETTLED, AND STAY as far under the radar as possible. Which wouldn't have been too hard considering the whole uniform requirement. I would have preferred black, but I was okay with the Navy blazer and white button-down. It was the ridiculously short burgundy skirt and the matching gold and burgundy tie that was going to take some getting used to. I couldn't wait for Xander to see me wearing it.

It *did* do wonders for my legs.

If I was being honest with myself, I wanted to be as hot on the outside as I was for him on the inside. I gladly embraced the last two hours of my sleepless night to rub one out, so I didn't resort to jumping his bones in the middle of the quad on day one.

After a quick online hair and makeup tutorial, I ended up arriving at the Edelberg Statue for my tour at a quarter to seven. Wild, loose curls and a light smoky eye accented a high-gloss lip. I was show-ready, only the show hadn't started yet.

While I waited, I took in my surroundings. The sun had

yet to shine the full extent of its light on the academy grounds. It was a huge, stony castle in comparison to my old schools. The trickling water display at the statue, the main tower of the Edelberg Building, and the two dorms branching from it, were a scene straight out of a book—an old, tattered first edition worth billions. It screamed money, like everything else about this little pinprick on the globe.

Mrs. Foster, the Student Outreach Liaison walked up ten minutes later. "How was your first night in the dormitory, dear?" In a crisp navy pantsuit with light makeup, tasteful gold jewelry, and her auburn hair pulled into a low bun, she was all business. She even walked with purpose, leading me through a side corridor to the library, seemingly ready to hurry and check me off her to-do list.

"Fine, thank you."

Since I was starting in the middle of the semester, I didn't get the usual student guide with side notes and social commentary, I got the abridged, need-to-know-only version. She wasted no time showing me the study halls, lecture halls, laboratories, and the amphitheater, before bypassing the girls' dorms—since I'd obviously already found my way there—and simply gesturing with a long, pointy finger at the boys' dorms.

"I trust you slept well?"

"Yes, thanks." I rushed to keep up with her, sweating despite the cool desert morning.

The halls were beginning to fill with students, and I found myself searching for Xander in the sea of faces.

"I'm surprised there were any available rooms. Who is your roommate?" She glanced back at me, only vague interest in her expression as we cornered into another corridor and entered the dining hall.

Apparently, the dorm room question was the rich equivalent of shooting the breeze.

"I don't have a roommate." I braced myself for a disapproving reaction much like Evelyn Gale's, but this was much worse.

Mrs. Foster stopped cold, her clacking heels skidding on the tile. "What room did you say you were in?" She drummed her fingers against her legs.

"214."

It was barely noticeable, but her shoulders tensed, and though she seemed like she was trying not to, Mrs. Foster gasped. Her expression turned severe, with tight lines and a sharp dip of her brows.

"That was—"

"What? What's wrong with my room?"

I searched her face, but she pressed her lips together and, as quickly as the flash of terror appeared, it was gone, smoothed away. She blinked, ironing out the creases in the faint crow's feet and heavy laugh lines. Again, her fidgety fingers pressed at an invisible wrinkle in her starched pants. My heart bottomed out and I made a mental note to buy a black light and gloves before going back to my room tonight.

"Nothing." She kept her eyes forward and forced a tight smile. "As I said, I'm surprised there was a room available." And that was the end of it, because she flipped her business mode switch back on. "Very good. Our first-year students usually sit there." She gestured toward two rows of tables in the far back corner. "But, even though this is your first year, since you're a senior, sit wherever you feel most at ease."

So, I guess I'll sit nowhere then.

An hour later, after she gave me a packet with a map and a list of facilities and emergency contacts, I was late into the dark lecture hall of my first period. Most of the seats were taken, but from my position at the door I spotted an empty one a few rows from the back and beelined for it. Except, right when I walked up, the guy on the end propped his long leg up on the back of the chair in front of him.

"Excuse me. Is anyone sitting there?" I whispered and nodded to the chair with all of his junk and flashed him a smile, to which he sighed dramatically. And loudly.

The professor was a youngish brunette with angry eyes, and thanks to Mr. Laidback, she zeroed in on me.

"Good of you to join us, Miss..." she trailed off, and I was freaking livid. All I wanted to do was sit down, stick my Airpods in, and get through the rest of the day until I could find out what the deal was with my room.

"Waters." I glared at the asshat.

At which point, I saw him flick his notebook to the floor. "Would you mind getting that for me, new girl?" His brow arched.

And so it begins.

I bent over to grab his notebook and... The lights. The snickers. The whistles sounding off along with a few other inappropriate noises about my ass, my pink lace panties, and getting me out of them. I'd completely forgotten about the skirt. I snapped upright and turned to the back of the room.

There was Xander with two other guys leaning on the wall beside the light switch. It was a complete dick move, but I shouldn't have been surprised that he still looked like an angel of darkness.

Just the sight of his tall, lean frame and his summery eyes sparkling over that cocky half-grin rattled my insides. I couldn't look at him without thinking about how he left me aching for more.

His eyes moved on me the way I wanted his hands to.

What the fuck is wrong with me?

It took me a second to come to terms with the fact that this wasn't a nightmare. This was the orchestrated prank by a bully and his peons. I knew just how to handle a bully.

I kicked asshat's leg and plowed my way into the row, tossing his junk to the floor and accidentally on purpose kicking his backpack under the chair in front of us. "Oops." I fluttered my lashes and pouted. "Sorry."

On the projector screen there was a slide with a pie graph sectioned in pink and blue with the words "supply and demand" bold at the top center. Thank goodness I studied the syllabus before I got there.

The professor pursed her lips and began this insane blinking glare. "Welcome, Ms. Waters. Please be on time to my class. I allow one tardy and then I begin to dock your grade." Her brows waggled for a slight second before she turned back to her computer. "Now, as I was saying, the factors of price regulations..."

Great.

I slouched back and fished out my laptop. It illuminated with my favorite picture of me and Honey Bun, my horse. I was just about to pull up a new document when a pen and paper slid onto my keyboard.

"Word to the wise, she hates bright screens and key-tapping." A bright-eyed girl with platinum blonde pigtails and sassy red glasses gave me an extra-wide grin. "By the way, I'm Abigail, Abbie, or Abbs, whatever. This is Owen." She leaned back far enough for me to see a cerebral-looking, slender black guy with lottery-luck bone structure and hazel eyes.

I waved and smiled, because after last night and just a few seconds ago, I needed some semblance of normalcy in the new, crazy world I'd been dropped into.

"Thanks," I mouthed. "I'm Izzy."

The rest of class was virtually uneventful, unless you counted some rustling in the row behind me and asshat at the end of the row dropping his phone in the middle of the lecture. Professor Evil glared at him this time. Which I found quite satisfying.

As the lights went up in a far less embarrassing display and everyone began filing out of the hall, I just sat there.

Even though I met Abbie and Owen, I needed less noise—less peopley interaction. This whole boarding part of boarding school was, like the damn skirt, going to take some getting used to.

"Not gonna lie, I'm starving." Abbie cracked her neck and faced me, but then her eyes darted right past me to the row behind us, and her mouth went slack. "Uh...well, we're going to go, but we'll meet you in the dining hall in five, Izzy."

"Okay, cool."

It took me a minute to pack away my stuff, but as the crowd ebbed away, my brain smiled its relief. I stood and stretched, then noticed I wasn't alone.

Xander and his two friends.

Right. Behind. Me.

"Oh. Hi," I said, tentatively. The word sort of hung out there, as awkward and tiny as I felt. My heart tripped around in my chest and every inch of my body clenched at the memory of him—his touch. Unsure what else to say, really, I just stood there. Nice seeing you again seemed too formal, and please finger fuck me again in the hall while our parents are in the next room didn't quite feel like it would cut it.

"Nice stems." His eyes darted to my legs then back to my mouth before meeting my gaze.

A tingling swept up the back of my neck, and I could feel a flush brush over my cheeks.

"Thanks." My heart was going haywire.

In the light of day, Xander Gale was even more of a perfect storm. He was sweeping long lashes over heavy-lidded eyes while doing his dark and brooding thing. He didn't even have to try because it just worked for him despite the preppy, clean lines of his uniform. He was made for the bad boy role, even in the middle of this pristine school—especially, even.

His friends were a little rougher around the edges, though.

The three of them were like the Neapolitan ice cream of boy bands with a delicious flavor to satisfy every girl's sexual fantasy. Xander's shimmery blond good looks were offset by one guy who gave me all the Clark Kent vibes with dark waves and stark blue eyes. On the other side was a guy, with decadent dark skin, a low-cut fade, and full lips.

As much as I wanted to hate and scoff at the way they were glaring at me, the heat in their eyes translated a little further south than my mouth.

Ah, the drought, yes. Still intact.

Xander cleared his throat, and I realized I'd been staring the whole time. I expected more from him. Maybe a wink or an easy nod, but I got nothing but deadpan from my gentleman of yesterday.

"Ok, well..." I said, hoping he'd fill the awkward silence, but he merely cocked his head and inspected me again. This time from head to toe.

I did my best to portray an easygoing manner with strong eye contact, pushing my shoulders back, chest out, chin high, but...nothing. On the inside, I was lightheaded, and my chest felt like it was closing in on me.

"Uh...'kay. Guess I'll see you later." Or not.

CHAPTER FOUR

XANDER

"It's been months. You're either up to it or not," Marshall said. His tone was matter-of-fact, but the bass in his voice echoed. He and Jorden were seated across from me at the dining table. Marshall's narrowed, icy blue eyes were fixed on the door. Unblinking, he chewed slowly, but the way he lifted his chin and bared his throat, I could tell his mind was made up.

"I'm itching to find out what this next one's got to offer," he said.

I tilted my head and peeked over my shoulder to see Izabelle Waters. She was standing in the middle of the dining hall, looking lost and alone.

Our eyes locked for a moment.

I swallowed and turned back to Marshall and Jorden, who were both zeroed in on her. The second they saw her in class, I knew she would be the one they chose. It was my fault. They noticed her because I'd been staring, couldn't take my eyes off her. That's when Marshall spotted me, and insisted we turn the overhead lights on her.

"I'm already on it." *Take the bait. Let me handle her.* "As a matter of fact, I laid the groundwork last night. She's not worth it."

Their eyes snapped to mine.

Jorden cocked his head at me, and a wicked grin played over his mouth. "What did you have in mind?"

"Hook, line, and fuck her. Toss her out with the rest of the trash in this wasteland." I bit my sandwich and chewed, careful not to meet Marshall's eyes. But I felt the weight of his stare. He knew how to read me like no one else. Sensed when I was lying. The perverse side of him reveled in my discomfort. And he homed in on more than lies and secrets. He sensed fresh blood and liked to draw it out.

"Is that so?" Marshall didn't seem impressed. I lifted my chin and threw my shoulders back while he studied me for a moment. "Innocent?"

"I dipped my fingers in for a taste. Tight and wet, but no."

He was salivating, and I knew it wouldn't be enough. "I want a souvenir," he said.

For Marshall Landers, my promise to fuck Izabelle Waters and leave her with the rest of the ruins wasn't sufficient. He wanted a keepsake. A memory to replay should he want to taste her for himself—a gentle reminder should she refuse.

I wasn't supposed to give a fuck about her, but I wanted the freedom to feel her out without the pressure of The Crows. I didn't want to share, and I didn't need the costly headache that went along with picking up souvenirs.

"Are we here again? I don't recall the last one going over so well with the administration." I felt my brow lift, challenging him. A mistake. "I'm just saying, if Yale doesn't happen, I'm stuck in this fucking place. I can't risk it."

"Xan, quit bringing up old shit." Ironically, despite Jorden Battle's complicit participation in our past ventures, he remained the peacemaker between me and Marshall.

Marshall straightened and flashed me a rigid smile as he pressed the air with his palms. "No. Xander's right," he said to Jorden without taking his eyes off me.

I crossed my arms and opened my mouth to protest, then stopped short.

The tension in Marshall's neck and shoulders was visible as his smile slipped. "Our last attempt to keep The Feed in line didn't fare well for us. As a matter of fact, I was just thinking. We should allow a new feed to come into our school and rule. Maybe let the administration tell The Crows what we can and cannot do."

On the table, I watched as he balled his fists and continued. "While we're at it, why not leave the innocent out in the meadow? Easy prey, huh, Xander? You know all about that, don't you?"

Heat roiled in my belly as I glared at him. I could feel my teeth grinding under the weight of my stiff jaw. Marshall didn't mince words. When I was too young and stupid to know about keeping your enemies close, I shared too much once. Or perhaps trusted the wrong crow with my father's little obsession.

Marshall didn't have to say it. The only acceptable option was to completely ruin Izabelle and capture the video proof in the process.

So that's how you want to play this?

I cracked my neck, the muscles quivering from holding back my anger. "Fine. I'll make sure she's at the party." I nodded and flipped around on the seat to face Izabelle, who glided toward me.

When she reached the table, I almost felt bad for her. She had no idea what was coming for her.

"Hi." She bit her lip and pushed a wayward curl behind her ear as she scanned the room. "I don't see my friends. Maybe I can eat with you and your friends?" She flashed a tentative, closed-teeth smile.

I looked her up and down, then refocused my gaze, wondering how long it would take her to get the message. *You don't belong here. We're not friends, you don't know me, and if you're smart, you'll keep walking.* But she didn't. She sucked in a breath and fidgeted, seemingly determined to reach me, appeal to my lighter side. I tried not to let my lips curl before turning my back on her.

She stood there for a few seconds longer then I heard the light click-clack of her shoes as she shuffled away.

"Nice work. I don't know what you're planning, but she better be at the Estrada—" Marshall said, but I didn't wait for him to finish his sentence.

"Or what?" I asked, just to fuck with him.

"Lovely. Death stares to go with my Greek salad." Honoré stalked up to the table, flanked on either side by the Harding twins. She twirled the tail of her blue-black braid in one hand holding her lunch in the other. "I really do prefer feta over American cheese." She flashed a glossy, tight-lipped smile and rolled her eyes as if we were boring her.

"Honoré, Penny, Nic. Always a pleasure." I addressed them in order of their Raven status, but my gaze was locked on Honoré. "I'm actually glad to see you." I paused briefly. "There's going to be a feeding."

For a split second, her emerald green eyes went wide as she gasped, then immediately smirked. "Do you have anyone in mind?" She seemed to have trouble swallowing.

The three of them crossed their arms in unison, while I let it sink in—let them sweat.

"Oh, please. By all means, do take you time." Penny, short for Penelope, the older of the sisters, tossed her glossy chestnut mane.

And of course, Nic, her echo, wouldn't be left out. She raised a thick, meticulously arched brow. "By all means."

As I regaled The Ravens with the details of the plan and their roles in it, I noted the sinister glint in their eyes. Fitting that a group of ravens is called an unkindness or a conspiracy.

Run while you can, Izabelle.

CHAPTER FIVE

IZZY

AFTER MY ELECTIVE PERIOD, ABBIE AND OWEN TRACKED me down on the way to the stables. I was kind of hoping the horses would cheer me up, because I wasn't in the best of moods after Xander basically pretended I didn't exist at lunch. Twenty-four hours was a new record—even for me. I'd let a hot guy with multiple personality disorder finger-bang and publicly reject me. It seemed I was destined to be an outsider my whole life, only this time I didn't have Dad to lean on.

"What happened to you earlier?" Abbie pushed her red glasses up onto the bridge of her nose and shuffled to keep up.

With his long legs, Owen was right on stride. "Yeah, we looked for you in the dining hall."

I sighed, twisted my hair into a massive bun, and stuck a pencil through it.

"Cute earrings," Abbie nodded toward my pair of purple topaz studs. "Birthstone?"

"Yeah, and my favorite color. Thanks. Anyway, about

lunch, let's just say I got a brief intro to this school's hierarchy."

"Let me guess. It wasn't a coincidence that The Crows were sitting behind us in Harding's class?" Abbie asked.

We whipped around a corner and exited the building out onto the west lawn. I could see the stables ahead, and the scent of fresh hay, sweat, and leather wafted toward us. The tension in my shoulders drained as I stopped and faced my two new friends.

"First of all, Crows? I don't even know what the deal is with this school. Sorry, academy." I held my palms up and shrugged. Gah, I hated how I was letting this place get to me. "Seriously, you two are like the only good things about being here. Since I arrived yesterday morning, it's just been crazy."

Both of them opened their mouths and shut them at the same time.

"What?" I asked, afraid to hear the answer, yet somehow I was aware I might need to hear it. I chewed my bottom lip and gripped my backpack straps.

Owen flipped his wrist to check the time. "It's three forty-three. Not enough time, but we have dinner and free time at five. Izzy, what room are you in?"

"Let's meet before dinner, though. If what you have to tell me is important, I don't want to wait. I'm in room 214."

Abbie dropped the pigtail she was fiddling with and her mouth went slack, her already pale skin, ashen.

"Okay, you guys are really scaring me. What's the deal with my room? Mrs. Foster reacted the exact same way when I told her."

Owen scrubbed a hand over his face before exhaling a winded sigh. "Fuck."

I was freaking out. I'd been half-joking when I thought about gloves and black lights after Mrs. Foster's reaction earlier, but now images of chalk lines and/or ghosts flashed through my mind. Everything around me felt like it was moving too quickly. My heartbeat raced, but I was frozen, rooted in place.

"Seriously, guys, you're scaring me. Should I be afraid?"

Abbie cringed and peeked at me out of one eye. "Not gonna lie. A little, but we'll meet you at the stables as soon as the period ends. We'll walk back to your room together. Don't freak out, but...do."

A few minutes later I'd changed my clothes and was officially shaking in my black riding boots. It wasn't like I could just waltz into the stables and the horses wouldn't sense it. I blew out a few cleansing breaths and tried to shake it off. Hay and gravelly dirt crunched under my feet as I made my way down to the last stall, where—I looked up at the name above the door—Jigsaw, a gorgeous pinto filly, was waiting for me.

"Well, hello." I reached out and gently brushed my fingers over her mane, but she pulled back. "Whoa. Don't worry. It's just today. I won't always be giving off the scary vibes."

I blew out a sigh and let my chin fall for a few seconds. When I peered up at Jigsaw, she seemed to sense, or smell, the shitty day on me. Next thing I knew, her fuzzy chin groove was on my shoulder. I leaned my head against her muzzle and rubbed her nose.

"I like you, too."

The rest of the period, I was still thinking about what Abbie and Owen needed to tell me, but my nerves calmed down...a little. Jigsaw and I exercised in the paddock, stretching her legs. Surprisingly, our rhythm synced quickly, and I relished the familiar comfort of her gait. My thighs straddling her, my feet in the stirrups, my hands easy on the reins, it soothed me. She felt like an old friend.

The best part? I never had to work to fit in, to belong, with the horses. No matter what place or school I was yanked out of or stuck into, home for me was always where the horses were. If the days got too rough here, I knew I'd feel safe in the stable.

After our exercise session, I led Jigsaw back into her stall. Once I'd removed her tack and given her coat a thorough grooming, I changed out of my riding clothes, found a stack of hay just off the barn, and waited for the students to leave and my friends to arrive.

"Let's be quick about this." Abbie let her backpack fall to the ground, settled on a bale of hay, and angled herself toward me while Owen followed suit. Based on her bouncing foot and the way he kept looking over his shoulder, I assumed they were risking something by letting me in on whatever it was they were about to share.

"How much do you know about Xander Gale?" Abbie asked.

I barely suppressed an annoyed sigh. "That's who all this is about? He's no one to me, really. My dad and his father served in Desert Storm together, so Xander's family is going to look out for me while Dad's deployed. That's mostly it..." I trailed off.

"Mostly?" Owen tilted his head and his mouth twisted into a smirk.

"We might have...kissed in the hallway at his parents' house last night, but it doesn't even matter, because apparently he doesn't even recognize me anymore."

Abbie dropped her face into her hands and shook her head. "Holy shit. Fuck."

"It wasn't that big of a deal, I promise."

Before I could say another word, Abbie dragged her backpack closer to her, unzipped it, and pulled out a history book. I must have looked confused because she held up a finger as she thumbed the pages until she reached about two thirds of the way through. At the top, the title read, "notes," and there was this organizational diagram that looked like a family tree or a hierarchy chart.

"What's that?" I leaned in for a closer look.

"Exactly what it says. It's my notes on this school and basically a guide to safely walking the line between feed and normalcy."

"Okay, you lost me."

Owen flipped the book around, so it was facing me, and proceeded to go over the school's players and non-players, or Crows, Ravens, The Feed, and the others.

Notes
Desert Badlands Wastelands Academy

The Crows (guys):
Xander Gale, Marshall Landers, and Jorden Battle

The Ravens (girls):
Honoré Montgomery, Penelope "Penny" Harding, and
Nicolette "Nic" or "Nickel" Harding

The Feed:
Emily Sutton, Clementine Olivier

The Others/Untouchables:
Abigail "Abbie" Edelberg, Owen Branch, Heather Devers,
Mischa Ferguson, and Ming Xhang.

"Is it time for Q&A yet? Because I'm lost. What does this even mean?" I asked. "And why are you guys untouchables?"

"My Dad is the dean," Owen stated.

Abbie shrugged. "I'm legacy. Abigail Edelberg," she dragged out the last name like I'd recognize it, and it did sound vaguely familiar, but then again, everything at the school was new to me. "As in the Edelberg building, statue...," she clarified.

At her raised brows, I nodded, trying to figure where I fit in this hierarchy. "So...if your families make you untouchable, where do I fit in?" I tugged at my collar. It was hot all of a sudden.

"Let's just say The Crows and Ravens are all legacies, and certain bloodlines make you untouchable," Owen added. And I did follow his deductive reasoning, but I was still trying to put the puzzle pieces together.

"Then what the hell is The Feed?"

Abigail eyed me tentatively, like she was apprehensive about letting me in on whatever it was she was holding back. She removed her glasses and her bright amber eyes dimmed. "I just wish we could have gotten to you first," she said.

"First?"

"If Xander already has his sights on you, there's not much we can do. I mean, we're your friends, and that won't change, but we can't be with you twenty-four seven."

"So...I'm The Feed, as in to be fed to The Crows and Ravens?"

They both nodded.

"Well, what are they going to do to me?" I eyed the page once more, but then my gaze snagged on the name with a line through it. "And who is Emily Sutton? Why is her name crossed out?"

I heard the horses neighing in the barn as I watched dust particles float in the waning sun.

For the next half hour, they gave me the abridged version of The Feed. Apparently, we, since I was lumped in with them, were not merely playthings. We were prey to be sought out, ruined both socially and sexually, and eventually thrown out of the Academy.

The Ravens, on the other hand, were not innocent bystanders. If The Crows needed anything, the Ravens helped them secure The Feed. They were equally dangerous, if not more so.

As for my other question, a year ago Emily Sutton was pegged. Each of The Crows, a mix of both current students and some who'd since graduated, took turns videoing themselves fucking her—a feeding. They didn't share the video initially. They held it over her head as insurance to keep her on the roster, but it fucked with her head and schoolwork, so she reported it to the dean. A horrible mistake. The Crows leaked the video and Emily killed herself in her room.

Room 214.

My room.

"Oh." I pressed a finger to my lip and bit down on it. "So, I'm fucked."

Abbie tugged both of her pigtails and slumped before straightening again hopefully. "Are you a virgin?"

"Um, I'm not sure why that matters, but no."

Owen considered this. "Does Xander think you are?"

I let my head hang back and thought about the conversation at dinner last night. How Mr. Gale asked me about a boyfriend back home. How Xander's fingers glided, hot and hard inside of me while my folds clenched tight around him.

"Probably."

Owen and Abbie shared a glance and she turned to me, something like hope in her eyes.

"Maybe, you'll only have to hook up with Xander. He's got a thing for virgins, and he might want to keep you for himself." She shrugged like that made all the difference. "I don't know, he's good-looking, built, and I haven't heard anyone complain."

As much as I wanted to hurl in my own mouth, the idea of fucking Xander didn't completely nauseate me. If I was being honest with myself, when he hustled me out of the dining room and into the entryway of Gale Manor, I wanted to feel the hardness in his pants working inside me up against the wall. Even with Dad in the other room, the threat of someone walking in on us had rattled something loose inside me and desire flared low and tight in my belly—then and now.

If that's what it took to keep from turning into Grand Central Station, trains being run on me day in and day out, well...so be it.

But for now, a new list ran through my head. One, avoid The Crows and Ravens at all costs, two, find out who the hell Clementine Olivier was, and three, find Emily Sutton's video. I needed to discover what I didn't know about Emily. Seeing the video would tell me exactly what I was dealing with.

Abbie, Owen, and I left the stables, ate dinner together at the dining hall, and finally, some time after seven that night, we made it to the girls' dorm. We were still laughing about the chalk lines and paranormal activity I envisioned after their first warning while I fished the key out of my blazer pocket.

"I literally wasn't planning to sleep," I giggled. But then their laughter ceased, and I turned to discover I wouldn't be sleeping alone tonight. "Hi, I'm—"

"Izabelle Waters. I know."

A pair of deep emerald eyes beamed back at me. They were lined all the way around with smudged charcoal and offset by thin, bright pink lips. Everything about her was flawless and expensive. Bluish black hair hung loosely over her slender shoulders in a side braid.

She was beautiful—and had moved into my dorm room, apparently. I took in her tailored leather bags and the bed across from mine fully dressed in dark grey sheets and a white down comforter.

I studied her for a second. "I was told I wouldn't have a roommate…"

"Mine, bless her heart—and my ears—likes to play the violin at all hours. Try sleeping through Concerto for Two Violins in D minor at three a.m. No thanks." She shook her head and flashed a pasted-on, toothy grin. "Anyway, when I heard you didn't have a roommate, I figured…"—she gave a coy, twinkly little shrug—"win-win for the both of us."

The three of us were all still standing there silent and slack-jawed, transfixed by the girl's spell. I thought it was just me at first, but the way they were watching her, both wide-eyed and ashen again, I was terrified to ask her name.

I didn't have to.

"I'm being rude. My name is Honoré Montgomery." Her delicate hand hung outstretched in the air while I picked my bottom lip up off the ground. She made a tiny noise that snapped me out of it.

"Oh, right." I slipped my hand in hers. *Shit.* "Nice to meet you."

It seemed The Feed was already being secured, and I'd have to wait to find Emily's video.

CHAPTER SIX

XANDER

THE COMMON ROOM WAS EMPTY OTHER THAN ONE OF THE Harding sisters in the corner watching YouTube on full blast on her phone. I'd come for the quiet, to lie back on the couch and kick up my feet in peace. I cracked my neck and blew out a frustrated breath as I read the same paragraph for the fifth time. Finally, I slammed the book shut and stretched my legs out in front of me.

"Can you not?" Penelope sucked her teeth and rolled her eyes.

She turned her back on me.

What the fuck is going on in this place?

A flash of anger settled in the pit of my stomach and I jolted upright. It seemed everyone was confused about who ruled this school. "Leave," I demanded. She glanced over at me, but there was no playfulness in my tone.

"Seriously, Xander?"

I felt my eyebrows lower and pinch together as I stalked over to her. Just standing there, I saw exactly what I needed to see. The tendons in her neck stood out, ragged pulse visible. Her eyes went wide and her body tensed as I gently wrapped my fingers around her throat.

"What was that you were saying?"

I relished the fear in her bright eyes as I tightened my grip, lifting her chin up, so she was forced to meet my gaze. The sight of her gasping for breath, clawing at my hands, begging for my forgiveness, it calmed me.

Or at least that what I needed her to think. What they all needed to see from me.

I closed my eyes for a second to hide from her agony, hating this mask I had to wear.

But this was what kept order. I imagined Penny retracing her steps, reconfiguring her flawed reasoning, trying to remember when she got so comfortable. The sensation of things moving too quickly to process—time running out.

"Maybe you don't want to be a Raven anymore. Maybe you're jealous and you want the attention that comes with being The Feed, huh? I see the way you watch Marshall."

Penny shook her head and tears welled in her bulging, reddened eyes. She gasped and I felt the lump in her throat move as she swallowed. She was shaking beneath the weight of my hand. I loosened my fingers. She was panting, gulping in as much air as she could, her chest heaving.

When she spoke again, her voice was a thick, hoarse whisper. "I'm sorry."

"What was that?"

"I said," she sobbed, "I'm sorry. I didn't mean to defy you."

A cool sensation of relief washed over me as I removed my hand from her throat and adjusted her collar to cover my fingerprints.

"Have I made myself clear?"

She got to her feet and moved toward the door, but as I

turned, she stopped. Her eyes widened as she stumbled back a few steps.

"Dining on twins might be a new and highly sought-after delicacy." My voice was even, but it was bolstered and ricocheted off the walls. The warning in my tone unmistakable.

The room fell silent.

I walked over to the window to look out over the west lawn. Light glowed from the stables, but I couldn't go there. The horses would know—sense the venom coursing through my veins. Still, I stared out longingly, missing the ease and comfort of being with a creature that shared an intuitive bond. No words necessary.

Spotting a silhouette moving toward me in the reflection, I heard heels clicking on the wooden floor. The shadow bathed in light revealed perfect posture, shoulders back, exposed neck, chin high.

An unkindness.

I remained silent, watching her in the glare.

"Ask and you shall receive," Honoré murmured.

I pivoted to her and studied her expression. It radiated superiority. Direct, probing eye contact. The beginnings of a smirk toying with her lips.

She moved a step closer, one arm crossed over her chest and the elbow of the other propped on it. "What?" she asked coquettishly, rubbing her pinky finger over her bottom lip.

"I can always count on you, can't I?"

"Absolutely." Then she huffed and rolled back on her heels, fidgeting with her necklace. "I saw Penny on the way in here. Did you have to do her like that?"

"'Uneasy lies the head that wears the crown.' It's high time we reminded everyone who runs this wasteland, and that includes any Raven bold enough to defy The Crows." I raked my hand through my hair and stared blankly at Honoré. I moved within inches, taking a wide stance, and looking down my nose at her. "Will Izabelle be at my party, or do I have to do everything myself?"

She didn't hesitate this time, but doubt bled through my faith in her. "I need a few days to work on her, but I'm sure she'll be there."

"Good. I wouldn't want to have to switch up The Feed."

CHAPTER SEVEN

IZZY

By Wednesday, I'd gotten good at dodging Crows and Ravens, except for Honoré, who made herself a mainstay of my morning routine before I slinked out of the room. Thanks to a few scenic side routes through the library and billiards hall between periods, and a strategic lunchtime disappearing act into the English lecture hall, the week was eerily uneventful. I got to eat mustard-soaked ham sandwiches in a dark room, safe and unbothered—the perfect place to watch a video no one wanted me to see.

I typed "Emily Sutton Desert Badlands death" into the search field.

The screen lit up with articles and images of what I assumed was her pre-Feed status face. The first one was her school picture. She was beautiful, with light brown hair pulled back with a gold and burgundy headband, warm honey eyes, and a full pout. She looked innocent and nice, which was saying a lot about anyone at this school. Every article included a quote from a friend or family member saying how she was an angel, funny, easy to talk to, and an all-around good person who they couldn't fathom ever taking her own life.

The headlines were blinding.

17-year-old Desert Badlands Girl Commits Suicide After Being Bullied

Girl Found Dead in Dorm at Desert Badlands

Nevada Girl, 17, Commits Suicide; Police Investigating Whether Bullying to Blame

Desert Badlands Academy Student Commits Suicide After Being Publicly Shamed by Boyfriend

Girl Kills Herself Because of Cyberbullying After Sex Tape Leaked

I wanted to stop. I was sick to my stomach. I didn't even know this girl and my eyes were filled with tears. What happened? Whoever did this to her, was it worth taking someone's life? She was someone's friend, someone's daughter... My mind snagged on that thought, and I shoved away the anger and the agony and kept digging.

I didn't know whether to be sad for this girl, or mad at her.

For the people who loved her. The ones she left behind to mourn and beat themselves up for not doing more, for not seeing the signs. People who sat around waiting for something to happen while they tallied the hurtful things they'd said or done. They panicked over every loved one left behind to make sure it didn't happen again.

It was a double-edged sword, with two parties to blame. I

wanted her to tell someone too. Let people know she was hurting. Give them a chance to help save her—figure out what they did wrong.

My brain was boiling as I cursed under my breath. I was mad at her *and* every damn one of the people who did nothing to help her.

I wanted Emily to reach out. I wanted her friends to know to look beyond the picture-perfect smile for the signs. I wanted the people doing the hurting to just stop.

"Shit."

Tears burned freely down my cheeks as I searched and finally, on some site which required me to confirm my age, I found the video. I swiped my tears away and pressed play.

The footage was shaky, but I could make out a bright hotel room. A girl—it wasn't Honoré, but she looked familiar —was guarding the door. And there was Sutton, on her hands and knees in a beautiful champagne-colored satin dress with spaghetti straps and her hair done up in a fancy prom chignon. She was deep-throating some guy.

Then suddenly, she stopped.

She was crying, and two black sludge streaks tracked down her cheeks.

"I don't want to anymore," she cried. "You said it was just going to be us. You said you loved me."

Who are you talking to?

"No one's making you do anything," the cameraman said. "You can leave whenever you want to, but what's done is done. Just one more for the birthday boy won't be the end of the world."

The camera wobbled and then a pair of hands propped it up. The heads were cut off, but the guy's body moved into view as he sat on the bed. He fiddled with his belt and zipper then freed himself from his pants. Emily took his full length in her mouth. He pressed on her head so she took him deeper as she sucked hard, her lips wide and thin around his cock.

It was only twenty-five seconds left on the video and my heart was racing as I watched in horror.

"Do it," someone whispered.

He pulled out, stroked his cock with fast, jerky moves with one hand while he yanked on her beautiful dress up and slid her panties down.

Ten seconds.

The guy didn't hesitate. He pulled her to her feet and traded places with her, only she was facedown on the bed. The instant he penetrated her the door opened, and a roar of cheers and applause erupted. Both hands now, he steadied her hips and pounded himself into Emily. Faster. Harder. More cheers, then chants.

"E-mi-ly! E-mi-ly! E-mi-ly!"

Two seconds.

"It's so fuckin' great to be a Crow."

I pushed the button on the top of my phone and the screen went black. I pressed it to my chest while the weight of Emily's Feeding riveted me in place. Fear and rage and terror crawled up in my throat. It slithered down into my chest and seized my heart. I wanted to weep for her and scream because of what they'd done to her. What she'd let them talk her into. I shook my head.

No way am I going to let that be me.

I jolted upright as the phone vibrated against my chest with a new message. I didn't recognize the 702 area code. Some part of me felt like it was The Crows watching me. Reluctantly, I opened the message.

Unknown: Evelyn and I are hoping to see you this Sunday. I'll bet a nice homemade meal would be just the ticket after your first week.

A spark of hope struck me.

Immediately, I remembered Xander Gale's parents, Quincy and Evelyn. At dinner she'd said to come to them if I needed help with anything, and after watching the video, all I could think was maybe they could get me out of the line of fire. I didn't have a plan, but I urgently needed to find a way out.

Mr. Gale wasn't the dean, so it technically wasn't snitching, even though he was on the board. He was the one who pushed for my mid-semester enrollment as a favor to Dad, based on the scholarship riding program. It was stupid, but I figured since he'd vouched for me once, maybe he'd put his neck on the line to protect his choice.

Then all I had to do was stick it out for a few months and it would all be over.

That's what I'd been thinking after Abbie told me about The Crows and The Ravens, how I just needed to find a way to peacefully coexist. But after seeing the video, I knew a few months in this wasteland was far too long, and their idea of coexisting was bullshit. My mind was all over the place as I wondered who I could and couldn't trust. The list was shrinking fast.

One thing was for sure. I wasn't going to be run out of school.

But Xander's warning not to tell his dad anything about me niggled in the back of my mind. There must have been some reason behind it, but at the moment I was leaning toward what seemed like the lesser evil. If I spoke to Xander's dad in private, it might keep me from being a meal for a murder of crows—at least for the weekend.

I bit my lip, debating what kind of response was appropriate, then tapped out a rapid-fire message. My fingers were still shaking, and before I could press send, I heard the creak of the floorboards and then light shone in from the door. I shaded my eyes, trying to see who it was, but the light was too bright. The person looked like a long, looming silhouette.

My voice was still shaky. "Um—"

"I don't think we've been properly introduced."

I jerked my head toward the male voice coming from the seat at the end of the aisle I was sitting in.

Marshall.

Fuck.

My heart knocked against my chest, and I could feel adrenaline storming through me. I clutched my backpack and considered running in the other direction, but as I glanced over my shoulder, there was Jorden Battle at the other end of the aisle, blocking me in. Oh, fuck. Fuck. Fuck. Fuck.

I swallowed and tried to steady my breathing, but it hitched up a notch, my chest rising and falling, panic paralyzing me from the inside out. This was it.

"I know who you are," I said despite my nerves. I meant to sound defiant and strong. I'd been through hell and back in my life, and I wasn't going to take this lying down—or on my knees.

"Like I said, we haven't been properly introduced. I know who you are, Izabelle, but I was rather hoping we could become friends like you are with Xander."

The glow of the light dimmed, and I looked over my shoulder again, praying it was someone I could plead to for help, but the silhouette came into focus. *Honoré.* I should have known.

I looked back at Marshall. "And if I say no?"

Marshall turned his head, facing forward and inhaled deeply before releasing a heavy sigh, getting to his feet. Slowly, he walked into the aisle and took the seat beside me. One of those crazy, missing-most-of-your-marbles smiles crept over his mouth and up to his eyes.

"Then I will make your life a *fucking* living hell."

I considered this. I expected this.

"What do you want? You want to run a train on me and post it online like you did with Emily Sutton?"

He still kept his eyes ahead, but the corner of his mouth tugged upward in a lopsided grin and a loud, boisterous laugh erupted from him.

"I like you. You don't beat around the bush." As he slid his hand up my thigh, his tone hardened. "Let me make this clear. You're beneath me. You don't belong here, but as long as you are here, I'm going to enjoy violating your comfort zone. If...and that's a very small if. If I want you, I will have you in any way I see fit."

He paused as if he didn't just send terror pulsing over my skin.

"Those dirty little lips of yours look like they're just my size. I've always wanted to know what it was like to fuck a black girl."

I crossed my arms, and he gripped my thighs, his fingers digging little half-moons into my skin.

"You're hurting me." I uncrossed my arms and pried at his fingers, but he held firm and tilted his head forward.

"I trust I'll see you at Xander's party, then?"

"Yes," I yielded. "Fine. I'll be there."

"Good. Make sure you dress accordingly. It's a lipstick party, so wear your favorite shade. You'll want to look nice for the camera." He fingered the amethyst charm on my necklace then let it drop with a dull thump against my chest. "Purple is one of my favorite colors too."

They left me in a crumpled ball of tears and anger and shame. I couldn't eat, my appetite was gone. I gathered my stuff and headed for the stables as I pulled my phone out, still trembling. All I knew was that I had one week to get away from Wastelands, and so far only one option for help presented himself.

Izzy: Sounds amazing, Mr. Gale. Thanks so much. See you guys Sunday.

CHAPTER EIGHT

XANDER

AS I FOLLOWED THE GRASSY PATH DOWN TO THE STABLES, my blood was boiling. I'd just left the squash court and run into Nic Harding, whose mouth spread unkindness just as effectively as her sister's. She fixed her thin red lips together and appeared to relish the news that Izabelle would be in attendance at my party next week. While she didn't provide further detail, she mentioned that Marshall had extended the invite.

It was all I needed to know.

I had to get to Izabelle, find out what Marshall said to her.

To my surprise, I made it to the stables first, which gave me a few minutes to get my nerves in check.

Months had passed since I was last here, since I felt the crush of fresh hay and dirt beneath my feet, the smell of earth and animal mixing. It was almost like coming home again. I'd almost forgotten how much I loved this place, the horses, the getting lost in the moment.

When your father decides law is your future, there's no sense in continuing to train to ride. I left it behind with all the rest of my childish dreams. Dad was intent on making me a man, and I was all right with it, so long as I didn't turn into the kind of fucked-up man he was.

I couldn't care less about a girl's so-called innocence. For me, fucking virgins was about giving them a chance. A girl could get over letting some guy her own age hit it when she was seventeen or eighteen. But there were lasting effects when some pedophile manipulated and conned his way into her panties.

That's where my head was at when I started all this shit with The Crows—I was stopping him, avoiding turning out like him.

Who was I kidding?

Knowing Marshall and what was coming for Izabelle, I couldn't fool myself anymore. I was exactly the same as my father. Like him, I was fucking virgins and stealing innocence.

Enough. I have to put an end to the feedings. I have to help Izabelle.

I walked the few feet to Rustin's stall and waited as he moved with his slow rocking gait toward me. A rush of home-sickness washed over me as I ran my palm over his coarse, rusty mane.

"Long time no see, stranger."

He released a happy neigh at the babying tone of my voice.

I looked up as the period bell rang and saw Izabelle rush past me in a blur. She didn't speak, just kept moving, head down, toward her horse's stall. She was still trying to maintain her distance, and I didn't blame her, not after an encounter with Marshall. He had a way of exerting his power over the weak.

Exactly what I was afraid of.

I glanced over as Izabelle grabbed a curry, rubbing it over the horse in a short, swift, circular motion to loosen the dirt and hair. Her hands worked in jerky moves, and even from a distance I could see she was trembling. The horse blew air out of her nostrils and let out a high-pitched squeal. Then Izabelle disappeared into the enclosure and I heard another squeal.

"Easy. I'm just going to check your hoof here."

I ambled over and peeked into the stall, my nerves shredding from just being near her. When Izabelle didn't immediately notice me, I cleared my throat to announce my presence. Her eyes darted up over her shoulder and she pressed her lips together in a slight grimace before turning back to the filly.

I guess I'm the last person you expected to see.

"I...um...came to see if I could help." I hated how my inflection went up like it was a question. "Not sure if you remember, but I used to train. I might be able to help."

"The farrier said he'll check her out tomorrow."

It took everything in me not to roll my eyes and tell her to get out of the way. It was obvious she just didn't want my help, and I deserved it. Still, I sighed and walked into the stall anyway.

Gently, I ran my hand over the point of the filly's shoulder to her ribs and back to her thigh, letting her get used to me. I was careful not to walk behind the horse as I bent down and gently lifted the back-right hoof. A foul stench saturated the air. The hoof was packed tight with hardened mud, and I noticed a deep, cracked groove between the heel, almost up to the hairline, where it was supposed to be teaspoon-shaped, fairly wide, and shallow.

I ran my finger over it. "May I borrow your pick?" I hedged around with my back toward her, held out my hand behind me, and let my eyes fall to her feet.

She hesitated, but then she placed it on my palm, lingering long enough for my skin to blaze beneath her touch.

That spark.

She'd given me a small taste, and now I was craving it, going through feverish withdrawals because of it. And Izabelle was the only one who could give me another dose.

This was the girl I met at the house. The one who sent shivers up my spine and filled my mind with dirty thoughts and lurid fantasies. I'm sure she thought I was an arrogant asshole—it was the persona I'd created to give me space. This was the same beautiful girl who made me want to kiss her and fuck her in the hall until she came on my fingers again.

That I could be a tyrannical headcase with the Harding sisters or anyone else who dared test me, and easy and gentle with her now, boggled my mind.

What was it about her?

"Suit yourself," she said. "I assume you retained some piece of information you think qualifies you to care for horses."

I smiled despite myself.

It's okay to take off the mask. I see you.

Behind her tough, defensive exterior, there was something more solid about her. She was real, hiding behind the storm. I realized Izabelle was the reason I couldn't run. Not from my father, and definitely not from Marshall. Because maybe there was something more to this girl.

Something worth protecting.

Maybe, if it was just us, I wouldn't mind defying the person I'd become.

The thought scared me. My fight or flight instincts kicked in, and almost every organ in my body urged me to spread my wings far and wide and ride the wind. My stubborn heart, though?

Fight for her, it said.

For a few minutes I worked the pick down the sides of the soft frog inside the filly's hoof, making sure there was nothing in the cleft, but as I cleared the black, pasty debris, the horse struggled to pull her leg free.

"How often do you clean her hooves?" I asked.

When Izabelle didn't respond, I turned to look at her. She folded her arms and flashed me a dismissive shrug.

"I'm only asking because it looks like your horse has thrush. It's pretty mushy and soft around the central sulcus, and it's sensitive and tender, which leads me to believe there's lameness. If the bacterial infection gets any more advanced, not only will it be painful, it could travel to the sensitive tissue and damage the healthy structure of her foot."

"Hence the reason I called the farrier, who'll let the veterinarian know. I'm sure they'll give her an astringent to kill the thrush. You don't need to worry about it." I noticed she'd edged closer to the door, her stance wider.

I nodded and chewed the inside of my cheek to keep from saying or doing anything to further put her on edge. "Listen, you don't have any reason to talk to me, but I need to know what Marshall said to you today."

Izabelle seemed shocked that I didn't already know. She swallowed and backed against the wall, her full lips twisting. "Why should I believe you? After what happened at your house...I thought." She swallowed. "I thought you liked me, but then you turned the lights on in class and treated me like shit in front of your friends. Twice. I know what you are. I know you're a Crow, and I know what you guys do, what happened to Emily Sutton."

"What did he say to you?" I felt my jaw tighten under the pressure of my gritted teeth.

Her eyes welled and she blinked back a wave of tears. Seeing the fear and the sadness in them, I hated that I had any part in making her a target.

"I'm part of The Feed. He wants me at your party, dressed for the camera. He wants to know what it's like to fuck a black girl." A tear fell and she quickly swiped it away. "That's what you want to do to me too, right?"

I stepped back, raking my fingers through my hair.

"No."

"So, then you finger-fuck every girl who comes to your house for the first time? I don't understand what this fucking place is. Or why all of sudden I have a roommate who's conspiring to take me down."

She inched closer to the door.

"Please. Don't be afraid of me. I'm not like them."

I don't want to be my Dad or Marshall. I know now that I've been going about this the wrong way, but I'm going to stop this shit.

I reached my hand out to her, then slowly pulled it back. The way word traveled at this school, it wouldn't be long before someone spelled out exactly what a lipstick party entailed. If I was going to convince her not to be there, I needed to earn her trust first. "I don't want to hurt you, but I don't want anyone else to either. Can we please just start over?"

"No." The word didn't match her actions. She just stood there, propped up against the stall, like she was waiting for me to make a liar out of her.

I slid the pad of my thumb over her bottom lip. Just like our time in the hallway, again her lips were swollen, and fire flared in her half-lidded eyes.

"I like you."

"What are you going to do to me?"

"What am I going to do *with* you? There are so many things I want to do *with* you."

My heartbeat raced, my breaths coming faster, but I moved closer still. My pulse quickened, and I watched the hint of a smile slip away.

"Xander?"

"I don't want to talk about it right now. Give me your phone."

She hesitated for a moment, but then she fished it out of her pocket and handed it to me, keeping her distance. I found her contacts and added myself before giving it back to her.

"For now, text me if you need me and I'll send you texts to keep you safe. We'll figure out something more permanent before the party next week." Before she could say a word to deter me, I brushed my lips over hers and left.

CHAPTER NINE

IZZY

By Friday The Crows and The Ravens had figured out all my hiding spots. Marshall's minions were posted at every corner, near the billiards hall, the library, the stables, and the lecture halls. They never looked directly at me, but I caught the side-eye stares and the slight head turns in my peripheral vision. I knew they were watching me because Xander was one of them.

Only he was on my side.

He'd been saving me all week, handing me off to Abbs or Owen, keeping Honoré at arm's length. Well, as much as possible, considering I lived with her.

Xander: Cinema is off-limits tonight. Common rooms too.

Izzy: My guardian angel.

Xander: I want to see you tonight. As soon as I ditch them, I'll text you. There's a place I want to show you.

"Someone's having a good day," Abbie said. "Anything you

want to tell me?" Her brows waggled as we squeezed past a loud-talking group of first-years and into the humanities building, heading to the girls' dorm.

I smiled and bit down on my lip. "Um...where's Owen?" I asked, squinting like I was really interested in the poster on the wall at my left. But then I read it and the bottom dropped out of my stomach.

My body felt like it was collapsing in on itself. My shoulders curled over my chest, and I began to shiver. My eyes and cheeks burned. Still, I couldn't stop staring at the poster. I was desperate to run and hide or back myself into a corner and pretend I wasn't falling apart in front of everyone.

"Izz? Are you okay?"

I couldn't look at her. I stared at the floor as I clutched my stomach. She grabbed me by the shoulders, and I felt like the weight of my body was dangling from her grip. Like if she let go, my legs would let me crumple to the floor.

I covered my face with my hands.

"What happened?" Her eyes flitted between me and the poster, but I still didn't have the words to explain. I was ashamed, humiliated. My skin crawled while my thoughts turned inward.

It wasn't one of those old ones with the big red corded landline phone and the word "HOTLINE" in bold. Not even the handprint in place of the O in "stop," or the noose. I was used to seeing those images. I'd trained my mind not replay every agonizing detail my mind saw when I came across them.

This one I wasn't prepared for. I didn't know how to handle something as simple as a bright semicolon. Even more were the words beneath it.

"You can choose not to end the sentence and go on."

It was a poster for the Suicide Prevention Hotline and the phone number.

The next thing I knew Abbie had called Owen and he was carrying me back to my room. When we got there, he lay me on my bed and tucked me under the covers. To fight the emptiness inside me, I curled in on myself, wrapping my arms around my knees. I was crying uncontrollably, trying to stifle the whimpers and sobs trapped in my throat, my mind and body numb and disconnected from each another.

I just wanted to close off my thoughts and wait for the pain to subside.

I'll just close my eyes for a second.

At the ping of my phone alerting me of a message, I snapped awake to find Abbie and Owen gone, and Honoré sitting up in bed, legs crossed at the ankles, watching me.

"So, I heard you literally broke down. Dramatic, much?" She quirked a smile, but nothing else on her face moved.

Other than Marshall, she was literally the last person I wanted to see. I was still nauseous and a bit dizzy when I sat up. I scrubbed a hand over my face and picked up my phone.

Xander: I need to see you. Sports closet. Back of the gym. 15 min.

"This isn't life or death. It's a party. A chance to break out some new lipstick. Any color you want." Honoré laughed despite herself, and rolled her eyes, hefting herself off the bed. She padded over to her closet.

For a few seconds, she rummaged inside for something, and I took the opportunity to peel myself out of the covers and plant my feet on the floor. I was still in my uniform, but there was no way in hell I would change with Honoré scrutinizing every move I made.

She peeked out at me before stretching her arm to fling a hanger with a purple dress on it toward me. "I know it's your favorite color."

I eyed the dark eggplant dress and short hem. "Thanks, but I'm on my way out."

Her brows arched, her piercing green eyes narrowed. "Meeting someone?"

"Just...meeting up with some friends."

"As if you have any."

I grabbed my jacket and a change of clothes, and didn't look back at her. "Don't wait up." As the door clicked shut behind me, I heard her scoff at the suggestion.

On the way to the gym I followed the path down the east lawn at the edge of Hepburn Creek. It was the long way, but no one was ever around so I didn't have to worry about The Crows.

I responded to the most recent of like ten group messages from Abbie and Owen, who were wondering what happened and if I was okay. They didn't press, but they said they were open ears when I was ready to talk.

I loved them for it.

Izzy: Can't talk now, but I'll call you as soon as I'm able. Don't worry. I'm okay.

Izzy: Thanks for worrying about me.

Abbie: That's what friends are for. Seriously, I'm here if you want to talk. If you don't feel comfortable talking in front of Raven Queen, you can always stay with me for the weekend.

Owen: She's alive! Hit me up whenever.

Izzy: I'm good for now, but thanks for offering. It means a lot to have you two. Talk soon.

The second Xander pulled up to the east entrance of the

gymnasium in a dark sports car, I felt a weight lift off me. I don't when or how it happened, but in the past two days, he'd become the center of my world, my anchor to reality. I wanted him on the deepest level, and I knew it the moment I saw him. He was the only person I wanted to let in.

CHAPTER TEN

XANDER

THE DARK, WINDING, SINGLE-LANE DESERT ROAD WAS shrouded in mist, but it came alive under the high beams of my headlights. Almost like we were in a tunnel, surrounded on all sides by crisp air and faint shadows outside the windows. It was like that for miles until I turned off at the exit and slowed the car to a stop.

"Where are we?" Izabelle asked.

I cut the ignition, got out, and rounded the trunk to open the door for her. "You'll see."

"Uh, should I be scared? You've got me out here in the middle of nowhere, it's pitch-black, and we're going into the woods."

"Just come on. I want to show you something."

Her eyes darted from me to the moonlight streaming through the tree branches, and I could tell when she noticed the cicadas droning nearby. I could almost hear the wheels turning in her head as she sighed and followed me.

To ease her nerves, I found her hand and took it in mine as we walked the few yards down the hilly slope until we reached the creek where our two best friends awaited us.

"I thought it might be nice to hang out with some old friends. You remember Rustin and Jigsaw." The horses shuffled toward Izabelle as she moved in wide strides toward them, her arms swinging, hair bouncing in the wind.

"I cannot believe you did this." She scratched her horse's mane and turned to me with a big grin beneath sparkling eyes. "Thank you. You don't know how much I needed this."

"I figured it might be nice to get away, take a night ride... and talk."

She didn't respond, but I took her silence as an accord while I inspected the horses' tack. I waited for her get up into the stirrups and checked to make sure the harness and saddle were secure before mounting my own horse and positioning my spotlight out in front of us.

We started out down the creek where the path was free of the uneven rocks and undergrowth.

As the trail widened, I loosened my grip on the reins and hung back a little so Izabelle could ride up alongside me. For a few minutes, I absorbed the quiet. No traffic or sounds of the city, just trickling water and the easy gait of hooves beating the path. The smell of pine and earth blended in a mix of freshness. I leaned my head back, inhaling as I watched the star-studded sky.

"This afternoon in the hall, was it about Marshall and the party, the feeding?" I glanced over at her, but she stared straight ahead. I guessed she knew this was coming.

Her hips rolled with the rhythm of the horse's movement. "No."

All day, I'd been fuming, thinking it was something to do with The Crows. It was why arranging this night away felt even more urgent than my need to get her alone. In the brush, I heard movement and crickets. The rush of the water seemed louder, faster, and I realized my senses were overwhelmed with the possibilities of what Izabelle might say.

"So then, what? People were saying you fainted, you had a nervous breakdown, and Owen Branch carried you back to your dorm. I didn't know what to think. Will you tell me?"

Suddenly, I was grateful for the cover of darkness. She couldn't see the tide of panic washing over me.

"Turn here," I said, nodding off to the right, where there was a clearing.

I was still waiting on edge for her answer as I tied the horses up to a tree and fished out a few things from my saddlebag. When we were stretched out on the blanket, our eyes trained on the stars, I found her hand and laced our fingers together. "You can tell me."

She pulled our hands to rest on her chest and I could feel her heart racing. She took her time, like every word was more difficult to say than the last. "It was a poster. Suicide prevention line."

I tightened my grip on her fingers and swallowed as her muscles tensed.

"When I was eight, my mom took her own life, and I really didn't get it. All I could think about was what I'd done wrong or how I could have been a better daughter. But I was also mad at her for leaving me, at my dad for living, and again, at myself for not seeing the signs."

"I'm sorry." My voice sounded strained and foreign to my own ears, genuinely apologetic.

"It's just...seeing that poster, it caught me off guard. I was humiliated..." She trailed off and breathed for a few seconds. "Have you ever felt like everyone could see right through you?"

"Yeah. All the time."

"In that moment, it was like everyone knew I couldn't save my mother." I could hear the emotion thick in her throat. "Especially since I'd just watched Emily's video. I read like a ton of articles about her and how her parents were so angry for all the same reasons I was—am—at my mom.

"When I saw the poster in the hall, I was right back there on the bathroom floor, scared to touch her icy skin and unmoving body, begging her to wake up. I read the words on the poster, line for line, and the next thing I knew I couldn't breathe or stand upright."

Izabelle shook her head.

"It's okay."

"I don't want to end up like them, like Emily Sutton. I'm so scared that I'm destined to wind up like my mother."

From the way her voice trembled, I recognized the toxic mix of fear and anger because I knew it well. I was two seconds away from telling her about Dad. How his actions and secrets changed me into this guarded, fucked-up monster. This dark person surrounded by an even darker circle of predators. I wanted to tell her, but when she turned on her side to face me and slowly grazed a finger over my lips, I knew I couldn't. Wouldn't. The same way Izabelle felt like her mother's fate had a hand in hers, I knew that no matter what I did, Dad's darkness would follow me.

I couldn't trust what the secret would do to Izabelle, to us.

What is she going to think of me when she knows what my Dad is?

Instead of detouring down that dead-end road, I leaned in and softly brushed my lips over hers. "I won't let them take you away from me," I whispered.

In the light I could see the tears streaming down her cheeks, and I recognized the desperate expression on her face. *Help me forget the pain,* it said. I kissed her again. This time, it was urgent and steeped with all the emotions swirling between us, the alchemy of it electrifying me. I deepened the kiss, pulling her taut against me, my tongue hungry and searching as I tasted her.

Izabelle ripped her mouth from mine. "I'm so mad at myself. These are the signs, and I'm ignoring them because I want you. So bad." She rolled over onto her back and scrubbed her hands over her face, pinching the bridge of her nose.

"What are you talking about?"

"Where is this going to go? I mean, how can you be two completely different people? At school we're ducking around corners hiding from The Crows. You have to ignore me, be fucking rude to me, so they don't know about us. And then there's this version of you." She sighed. "This sweet and tender guy who's so careful with my feelings, who takes me on amazing starlit horseback rides out of the blue. You're gentle when I need you to be, then so maddeningly rough I just want to hate-fuck your brains out and then crawl into a corner and cry. Why can't it just be normal?"

"I know."

I did.

I wanted it, too. The normalcy. The regular worries people our age overreacted to...grades, college, arguments with our parents about staying out late. I wanted that. Not checking my father's desk to find his next target. Not humiliating girls in hotel rooms. I was just as bad as Dad and Marshall, no matter how much I didn't want to be.

I propped up on my elbow so I could look into her eyes. "Promise me you won't give up on me—you'll let me prove I'm different."

Izabelle climbed on top of me, thighs hugging my sides, then leaned down and laid a tender, sexy kiss on me. She was shivering while she ground herself on my dick.

I twisted and laid her on her back, positioning myself between her legs, then sweeping a curl out of her face and kissing away each of her tears. Every nerve ending in my body stirred and tingled as warmth flooded my chest. She stared up at me with glossy, half-lidded eyes, her arms akimbo and wild coils scattered around her head on the blanket as she slightly parted her legs.

"I want you," I said, leaning in to nibble her bottom lip. I was drowning in need, but I held back against every raging, savage instinct embedded in my genes. I was of my father, but I didn't have to *be* him.

Her chest rose and fell with shallow, hurried breaths, but her gaze was fixed on me.

"Then have me."

I was mesmerized by the way she arched her back, writhing beneath me, torturing me. It was all I needed to hear. I scooted back, peeled off her panties one leg at a time, dipping my fingers inside her.

She hissed, and the sound only electrified my need.

"You're already wet for me."

Izabelle pulled her bottom lip between her teeth and squeezed her thighs together against my hand.

"I want to feel you moving inside me," she whispered and moaned.

As she squirmed, I groaned and freed my dick from my pants, stroking it while I fished out a condom and glided it down my shaft. I was wholly consumed as I buried myself inside her and felt the walls of her pussy clench around me. A surge of heat coursed through me as she bucked and tied her legs around my waist, forcing me deeper.

"Fuck, you feel so good."

Every move and every whimpering sound she made was so fucking hot.

I tugged her shirt up over her bra and yanked the cups down. The soft curves of her breasts and the small brown nipples teased me. I took one between my teeth and grazed the tender skin. I sucked it and licked, hungry but still unfulfilled.

It was like I couldn't get enough. I couldn't get close enough. She was this addictive high I couldn't match with anyone or anything else. I was inside of her, but she invaded me in every way. She was on my mind and in my heart every second of the day, even though I never invited her in. When I wasn't with her, I was thinking about her, texting her all hours of the day, wondering what she was doing and when I could see her again.

This was more than sex.

"Don't let them hurt me," I heard her whisper.

As much as I was enjoying this, my heart wouldn't let me forget how my addiction made her a target. I hated who it made me. More than anything, I didn't want to taint the person she made me want to be.

With both hands, I gripped her hips and slammed harder and deeper until her body quaked and quivered under me.

Then, I let go.

CHAPTER ELEVEN

IZZY

SATURDAY XANDER AND I WERE TUCKED AWAY IN A HOTEL a couple of towns away. We slept, had mind-blowing sex, ordered takeout, had sex again, watched two seasons of *Paranormal Ghosthunters* on his phone, and now we were just lying in bed breathing. I knew we were thinking about the same thing. The weekend was almost over. Come Monday, we'd be back at school, another day closer to Friday.

Doomsday.

"Next week is Valentine's Day," he said out of the blue, and a giggle bubbled up inside me.

We were thinking about the same day from opposite ends of the spectrum. I'd thought about it nonstop, the irony. How a day meant to celebrate love was going to be marked with so much hate.

"I know. It's your birthday."

"I'm serious. I want to buy you something special. Maybe something in your favorite color." He nodded to the small amethyst pendant on a thin gold chain around my neck.

"It's a gift from my Dad."

"Is it your birthstone, too?"

I squinted at him, working my way around his thought process. "Yeah. It's the twenty-seventh. But these"—I tilted my head to the side and combed my hair out of the way to show him my earrings— "they're not amethyst. Topaz. I really just love the color purple. It's me and my dad's thing. He brings me back something purple from everywhere he's stationed or visits."

Xander turned on his side and propped himself up on his elbow. Affection glowed in his summery, blueish-green eyes. "What if I cancelled the party and took you somewhere, just the two of us?" I could hear the hope in his voice, and I hated to drown it out.

"Nothing will change but the date," I said. "If Marshall is as malicious as I believe he is, cancelling the party will only make what he does to me that much worse. I just wish I could find a way to take his sights off me. Either ruin him or..." I trailed off because even saying my thought aloud worried me about my own moral compass.

"Or what?" Xander pressed.

"What if someone was else took my place in the feeding?"

Even as I said it, I hated myself for wanting another girl to go through my worst nightmare. But, somehow, I felt like the answer was under the last stone I'd left unturned. I'd gotten distracted with the video of Emily and seeing the poster, then getting swept up in Xander this weekend, but I'd meant to keep digging.

"What are you thinking?" Relief suffused his features as he looked at me. At this point, I could tell we were both ready to latch onto any alternative.

I sighed and finally met his gaze. "Who's Clementine Olivier?"

For the next several minutes Xander unloaded the whole scoop about her. She was a second-year who got pegged for a feeding last semester, but before Marshall could roll out his plan to defile her at a debutante party, she got her hands on Emily Sutton's original video—the one taken from his phone, and flipped the script on him, thus saving herself. It didn't remove her from The Feed, but until Marshall could figure out how he was going to get his revenge, he let her slide.

"So, he's basically just lying low, waiting for her slip up?"

Xander nodded and shrugged.

"And what's his deal with always doing it at a party? He just needs his cronies around to boost his ego, or is it to make everyone else accomplices by their presence alone? He's so fucking wretched."

"At least that's what he tells you. If you're there and you didn't do anything to stop it, you're culpable."

I rolled my eyes and sighed. "I'm so over this guy. What a grade A douchebag. He thinks he's some CSI detective, outsmarting his lowly peons, and everyone just falls at his feet, lets him do whatever and get away with whatever. I don't know who she is, but I'm liking this Clementine girl more by the second."

Xander plopped back down on the pillows and raked his fingers through his hair. His voice came from somewhere far off. "What if we just skipped everything and ran away? I get away from my dad and you avoid Marshall."

The idea had crossed my mind a million in one and times, but I didn't have money like these kids. No one was going to pay for my college tuition. I needed the riding program. The scholarship to Colorado State was contingent on my grades here and the experience I was getting by shadowing the farriers and vets. I couldn't pass that up, and I refused to let Dad down.

"That's not an option. My scholarship is riding on this semester at Badlands."

My blood boiled. I hated how a handful of fucked-up kids

could affect my future. The more I thought about it, the more the idea of letting them get away with it pissed me off.

Xander's slightly amused tone snapped me to. "Mind telling me why your face looks like you want to choke someone out?"

I cut my eyes to him, and he slipped his thumb into my mouth, commanded me to suck it, and I didn't object. Mostly because it was hot as fuck feeling any part of him moving on my tongue. He pulled out and pushed it back in. Over and again he did this. Each time, I was more turned on.

With his free hand, he pressed his fingers between my thighs, rubbing the throbbing ache, slow at first. Then fast and hard until my back arched, and I shoved my pelvis hard against his hand. I was panting, moaning. Fire blazed all over my skin. In the moment there wasn't anything I wouldn't have done to get him to release me from my misery, but then he pulled away.

"Why'd you stop?"

"I want you to take your anger out on me."

The bad boys are always the kinkiest.

I considered his request for a brief moment before I realized how hot hate-sex is. I arched an "are you sure you want me in control?" brow at him and he responded by stretching his long frame over the length of the bed.

Now this I could get used to.

"Oh, you are so in for it."

I climbed on top of him, drawing my shoulders back. His eyes darted to my mouth, then up to my eyes, and a wave of heat washed over me. My pulse and my breaths quickened at the idea of him lying beneath me, ready for whatever I wanted to do to him.

His hazy eyes crinkled at the corners. "Is that it?"

This made us both laugh because I was just sitting there, my mind going haywire, but my body was stiff as a rail, completely content to just stare at him. He was beautiful, and damaged, but I didn't care. I found myself lost in the plans we were making, imagining a future together, and I realized as my heart tripped around in my chest, I was falling for him.

A slow and sexy smile grew on Xander's face and his blush deepened, but his warm eyes pinned me in place. He pushed up off his elbows and drew me into a sensual, hungry kiss. I was boneless, grappling with the weight of my heart.

"Me too," he rasped.

I didn't have to say it. He knew. By his longing expression, I could tell he felt it too.

Gently, taking his time, he kissed down the curve of my cheek to my neck, letting the pads of his fingers swirl in circles on my bare back. When he reached my breasts, his tongue blazed over the sensitive skin and he lifted my hips and positioned his length for me to slide down onto it. We rocked to a steady rhythm, saying with our bodies the words I couldn't. I rolled my hips, relishing the feel of him inside me. We were one, and my walls were coming down faster with every touch.

"This probably sounds crazy, but I don't want to be without you," he said, and it pushed me over the edge, because the words were coming out of his mouth, but they were my thoughts.

I rode the orgasm, releasing a sharp cry because it was too much too soon. How was it even possible to care this much about someone in less than a week?

It can't be real.

But every inch of my aching body in his strong arms knew it was.

CHAPTER TWELVE

XANDER

The next morning, I woke before Izabelle. In the quiet sun, I slipped out into the hall and waited for the next elevator, headed for hotel registration to pay for the incidentals and request a noon checkout so she could sleep longer. We'd spent the rest of the night in a fog of sex and bliss. We never did say the words, but I knew we were on the same page—falling hard and fast.

But as unromantic as it sounded, I just couldn't help worrying that plummeting at that speed with so much force might leave us broken.

I watched the elevator floor numbers illuminate above the doors. We were on ten, but the car had been stuck on twelve for a while. I checked my watch. Nine forty-five. Checkout was at eleven. I peeked up at the glowing numbers again and decided the stairs wouldn't be so bad. The faster I got this done, the faster I could get back to bed.

When I exited the stairwell, I peeked over at the elevator and shook my head. It was finally on ten.

Too little too late.

The line was empty at hotel registration, so I got in and

out in minutes, but as I looked up and saw the gift shop, something in the window caught my attention.

"Good morning. Is there anything I can help you with, dear?" An older woman with short salt and pepper hair and tortoiseshell glasses beamed at me. She had kind brown eyes, and her smile seemed genuine. I was probably her first customer of the morning, considering the hotel wasn't in a prime location near any landmarks or airports. Precisely why I picked it.

"Hi. I saw a figurine in the window display. Should I get that one, or do you have any in the back?"

"Which one was it? The heart, maybe?" She winked and a knowing grin tugged at the corners of her thin lips. Everything about her expression said *I saw you with your lady friend*.

I assumed as much. When Izabelle and I came down to dinner last night, all eyes were on us. I guessed it's what we got for setting foot into a small town where nothing ever happened. Anything and anyone new winded up being the hottest topic of conversation.

"Actually..." I walked over to the window and grabbed the display. "This is the one I was talking about."

"Ah, the filly. She's just adorable." She gently pinched her thumb and forefinger together to take the small brown glass horse from my hand. "I have the whole set. A new one comes out every year, and my girls love horses, so I put two to the side for them as soon as they deliver 'em. You lucked out. This is one of the last two."

The store clerk went into a backroom and grabbed the one in its box and rang me up. I thanked her for her help and walked back toward the elevator with an extra spring in my step. It surprised me how I felt compelled to do something for Izabelle. I'd never wanted to give or buy anything for a girl. It was confirmation of my feelings for her.

No surprise, the old elevator was still working its way to

the lobby, but I decided to wait for it since it was on the second floor. When it pinged and the doors finally slid open, I corrected my posture and lifted my chin, steeling myself. I didn't speak first.

"Gale, what are you doing here?" Jorden asked.

"Yeah, are you here by yourself?" Nic added.

I tilted my head and surveyed their disheveled clothes, missed buttons, and the smear of Nic's lipstick.

Why get a room when there's a perfectly good elevator?

"Hey...who all's here?" I asked, less concerned about these two than Marshall, Honoré, or Penny. Jorden was a Crow for sure, but he was subtler about his command tactics. And Nic? I never worried about her. The Harding twins were tight when they faced a common enemy, but when pitted against each other, the sharp claws came out, and Penny usually ended up on top. Nic was so hungry for any spotlight her sister wasn't already basking in, she would do anything to win a Crow over.

"Oh, it's just us. We came to check out the...sights." They both laughed, but the lip-bite Nic flashed Jorden as she said it was all the confirmation I needed. We both knew the sole selling point for this place was its obscurity.

"Here's the thing," I started...but for the life of me I couldn't come up with a believable lie. "I came up here to get away for the weekend." It was a shit attempt, but I glared at them. In other words, *it's none of your fucking business what I'm doing here. Don't ask, and for damn sure, don't fucking tell anyone.*

"Yeah, okay, cool. Well...it was good seeing you," Nic fumbled over her words, her eyes flitting from me to Jorden, clearly unsure where her loyalties should lie at the moment.

"All right, my dude. You good?" It was that throaty, under-handed tone. He could give a fuck if I was good, but it was a show of force—a veiled threat hidden behind social platitudes.

I felt my jaw tighten from the pressure of my clenched teeth. "I'm good."

Jorden glanced at the box in my hands and nodded. The corners of his mouth pulled down, and his bottom lip pushed out as he swiped his finger under his nose. "Cool." He scrutinized me from head to toe as I entered the elevator. "Come on, Nic. Let's go watch Marshall's *video* again."

"What video?" I straight-armed the doors. My breath caught in my throat and my stomach hardened as I searched Jorden's face. He was all crinkly eyes and wicked grin.

"I thought you knew."

"Knew what?" At my temple I felt a vein throbbing as fire seared through me. I could've wrapped my bare hands around his throat and ended him right there, but I needed to know what he wasn't telling me—what Marshall was up to.

I stepped out of the elevator and stood between them. "Show me." When they both stood there, neither one moving to take out their phones, I flexed. "Now."

Jorden was the one to jam his hand in his pocket and pull his out first. When he put his thumb on the button, the screen glowed to life and he pulled up his photos. The most recent one was dark, but in the middle of it, there was a triangle, indicating it was a video. I glowered at Jorden and pressed it.

At first, I wasn't sure what it was until I heard the horses in the background.

What the fuck?

My nerves felt raw beneath my tense muscles. My heart plummeted. "What is this? Marshall followed me?"

On the screen, Izabelle and I were on the blanket beneath the stars, her legs wrapped around me as she bucked and pulled me tighter. The camera zoomed in so close I could see my dick plunging inside her. Then, "Fuck, you feel so good," I heard myself say.

I tried to look away. I didn't know what to do. I was both humiliated and raging.

"Don't turn away yet, you'll miss the best part," Jorden said.

I kept swallowing. My throat was dry from my rushed breathing as I watched us. I'd freed Izabelle's breasts and I was sucking on her nipples, teasing them as I glided in and out of her, falling, when she said, "Don't let them hurt me—"

They heard everything.

Jorden closed the video, and my eyes went wide, but despite my clouded vision I stared him down.

"I have to tell you, man, that's some cake shit, right there. Sweet. I wasn't sure I wanted to fuck her before. Now that the trailer is out, though, I might be first in line."

"Fuck you." I bared my teeth and barreled toward him with a guttural roar as I grabbed him by the throat. With both hands cuffed around his corded neck, my strength felt Herculean. I wasn't thinking, I was reacting in the most visceral, feral way possible. Every muscle and vein strained against my skin. I was completely losing my shit. Spittle building up in the corners of my mouth. My body shaking as I dug my nails deeper, breaking skin along the back of his neck. I was on a ledge, twitching, adrenaline coursing through me.

My lips were a whisper's distance from his ear, but all I heard was my heart pounding in my ears and the feel of my pulse skyrocketing. "I. Will. Kill. You," I growled.

I felt the dozen or so pairs of eyes on me before the slaps on my back and the yanking of my arms pulling me off of Jorden. He wheezed and coughed, but the sinister glare and the smirk were still there. What's worse, Jorden flitted a glance over my shoulder, and I didn't have to look to know Izabelle was right behind me.

CHAPTER THIRTEEN

IZZY

"What the hell was that all about?" I asked, the second we got into the car.

He'd glared at me twice and apologized three times, but we'd agreed we wouldn't talk about it until we got out of the hotel.

"Okay, we're out, now can you tell me what they were doing at the hotel and why you could've cut steel with the death stare you were giving Jorden?"

Xander's eyes were trained on the road, and he was going at least twenty over the speed limit, but he still didn't look at me.

"What did he say?" I pressed. My eyes darted out the windows on all sides of the car. Nothing but dusty desert sprawled around us, and I was none the wiser about where we were. Xander clearly had a destination in mind, but he didn't share it with me. "And where are we going? This isn't the way back to Badlands."

"We're not going back," he said. Everything about his tone sounded dangerous.

"You're scaring me. Talk to me."

This caught his attention, and finally he glanced over at me, and it all made sense. I shifted on the seat to face him. I'd been studying his profile every second since we met, but I missed this facet of him.

"They have something on you, don't they?" I asked. "Marshall knows you've been helping me. He knows we've been together all weekend, and he sent Jorden to do his dirty work."

Xander didn't confirm or deny. He just glanced at me, and for a second I got a glimpse of a lost boy who so badly wanted to do the right thing by people, but somehow got dragged into the hurt and came out damaged on the other end.

"I'm right." I shook my head and let my chin rest on my chest, my shoulders slumped at my sides. I'd been reading the signs all wrong. They weren't about me. Yes, Marshall was targeting me and using me, but to get to Xander. It was all a game. Two kings fighting for a throne.

When I lifted my eyes again, he looked defeated, devastated.

"What happened between you and Marshall—"

"They have a video." He cut me off as he veered into the curve of the road, and I turned back to him. His jaw was tight, and there was a slight twitch that let on he was clenching his teeth.

I felt my brows knot. "I know. I told you I saw it. The Emily Sutton one, right?"

He tightened his grip on the steering wheel and the same expression he aimed at Jorden was back. "Of. Us," he said sharply, his voice thundering through the car. "They followed us. Last night under the stars, they recorded us."

"I'm sure he's lying. They just hate us being together. And anyway, it was super-dark, and I didn't see anyone."

He laughed at this. "I saw the video. I saw us making..." He blinked and inhaled, shaking his head. "Marshall Landers does not make veiled threats. He's going to use the video to get whatever the fuck he wants."

No words came out of my mouth. I considered the anger in Xander's tone and the chances of Jorden and Nic showing up in the same deserted hotel. All over again, I felt Marshall's hand squeezing my thigh in the dark lecture hall, his demand that I be at the party. Then there was Xander, showing up randomly in the stables. I scooted back against the seat, laid my head on the crossbody seatbelt, and stared unseeing out the window for the rest of the drive.

With every bend of the road, my eyes welled, and tears streamed down my cheeks.

I'm so stupid.

This...this whole charade with Xander, it was a setup. The dinner at his parents', his help avoiding The Crows, this entire weekend getaway. They were small glints of light in the darkness and I'd walked right into the fire. From the beginning, Abbie and Owen had warned me about Xander, about The Crows. With my own eyes I saw the hierarchy, and I should've known my place, but I was too eager to find some sort of silver lining.

It was all a trap to get me to the party by any means necessary.

From the shadows of the car, I watched him. The sharp lines of his jaw, the piercing blue-green eyes, and the almost sculpted, regal way he held his head, chin up, throat bare. He was the irresistibly handsome king of The Crows, and Marshall might be bad, but he was only challenging Xander for the throne.

Xander glanced over at me, and he must have registered my thoughts by the expression on my face, or the way my chest rose and fell rapidly, because his eyes softened. He reached his free hand out to take mine, but I jerked it away.

"No."

My tears kept coming as I slowly shook my head and swallowed. "Don't. I can't believe I trusted you."

"What are you talking about? Don't do this, Izzy."

I gasped because he never called me by my nickname. "See? I knew it. You've never called me Izzy. In fact, I specifically remember you telling me you didn't care for it, and now you're... You're just like them. Or, should I say they're just like you?"

"I didn't have anything to do with this. I promise. Please, you have to believe." His voice was shaky, and he kept looking from me back to the road. "I would never do this to you. I care about you. I wanted to protect you from them." He paused. "I'm falling for you."

"Yeah, sure."

Silence fell over both of us, because as much I was afraid to believe him, I heard the hitch in his voice. I wasn't expecting "I'm falling for you." I wasn't expecting his heart to be out there on his sleeve. I thought maybe we'd yell for a few minutes and I'd tell him to take me back to my dorm, but this? I couldn't keep tiptoeing around it.

I felt my eyes go wide and I must've been breathing, but I couldn't hear anything over the sound of my heartbeat knocking in my ears.

"I—"

"Don't say it if you don't mean it."

I wasn't going to tell him I was falling, too. I was going to tell him how hurt I was, but then his mouth set in a smooth line and he turned his eyes away. The road unraveled into a straightaway in front of us and the moment was lost. We didn't speak again for the rest of the drive.

All I could think about was that Xander Gale was falling for me, not the fact that my life was officially over. There was no coming out of this unscathed. If Dad saw the video, or the admissions office at CSU, my future would be shut down. By the same token, if Marshall got what he wanted from me... I didn't know what it would do to me, to who I was. I couldn't guarantee I'd be the same person on the other side.

Would I end up like Mom or Emily?

My body felt heavy, and everything seemed to be moving in slow motion. After Mom died, I kept myself going by being strong for Dad. Now he was off on his tour and probably not even thinking about me. I didn't have anyone to keep going for. It was the first time I understood Mom and what she was likely going through a little better. It just seemed so much easier for everyone to take me out of the equation.

I want to die.

As the car came to a stop, my eyes snapped up to the windshield.

Gale Manor.

"We can spend the rest of the day here. We'll figure out the rest later." Xander said as I flashed him a small smile.

Later.

Even if I was devastated, at least there was still today.

CHAPTER FOURTEEN

XANDER

I GOT OUT OF THE CAR BEFORE IZABELLE AND ROUNDED THE hood to open her door. As she stepped out, I plastered on a smile for her sake, but I was low, my heart somewhere in my stomach. A stab of resentment flared in my gut.

How could she fucking believe I had anything to do with Marshall's video?

This whole thing sent me spinning into a full-fledged panic, and I knew anything I said would ring hollow, so I reined it in for Izabelle's sake.

"Listen," I squared her shoulders to me and tipped her chin up with my finger. "I need you to know I had nothing to do with the video." I stared into her warm brown eyes, begging her to believe me. I knew wounded indignation laced my tone. I didn't mean to blurt it out, but every word I said in the car was the truth.

She blinked back her tears. "How can I know that, huh? How can I trust you, since I know everything I've been warned about The Crows is true?"

"I'm going to protect..." I trailed off as the grainy image of the video flashed across my mind, a blaring reminder of how I'd already failed to protect her once. I stroked her arms. "I've got some ideas for what to do, but for now, it's Sunday, so let's just enjoy the rest of this weekend."

"Okay."

Her voice was so tiny. I drew her into a kiss, letting my tongue slip into her hot, wet mouth. I pulled her bottom lip between my teeth and sucked before seeking and finding her tongue again, dipping my fingers into the waistband of her black leggings. I could've fucked her right there in the driveway, but then I heard the faint squeak of the front door opening.

"I'm so glad you could make it, Izabelle."

My jaw tightened under the grinding of my teeth as I turned and glared at my father.

"Xander, I wasn't expecting to see you this weekend."

"What are you talking about, you're glad she could make it, Dad? She isn't here to see you." I jerked my eyes away to meet Izabelle's sheepish gaze. "What is he is talking about? I thought I told you to stay away from my father." The last few words came out low and hushed as I bore into her.

She bit her bottom lip. "He, uh, texted and invited me over for dinner with him and your mom to celebrate my first week. It was Wednesday, before I talked to you in the stables. I didn't think it would be such a big deal."

"Of course you didn't." My voice thundered and I hated the bitterness in my tone. I inhaled a cleansing breath before speaking again. "You cannot trust everyone you meet—"

"But, it's your dad. I didn't know it would be a thing."

"Well, it is."

I twined our fingers together and turned on my heel to lead her to the front door, where my father stood waiting for us. He looked just as pissed to see me as I was him. It was obvious I'd foiled his little plan to get Izabelle alone, but we both knew this wasn't going to be his only attempt.

"We'll be in my room if you need me," I said, brushing my shoulder against his as we passed. "We won't be staying for dinner. I'm sure you and Mom will be fine without us."

When we made it upstairs to my room, my blood was boiling, and I knew what I needed to do. My fucking father was a hunter. Once his sights were on his target, he wasn't going to give up unless someone else got to his prey before him. His invitation to Izabelle was proof of his plan—the game to lure in an innocent and sacrifice her to his fetish, but I couldn't let it happen.

I closed and locked the door behind Izabelle.

She was just standing in the middle of the room, gawking open-mouthed at the vast space, and the perfectly curated, muted navy blues and grays with sturdy, industrial metals and wood.

"Lie down on the bed," I commanded, tugging the sleeves of my jacket and letting it fall to the floor where I stood.

Izabelle looked both shocked and turned on at the same time. "What, here?" She waggled her brows. "But your parents are downstairs..."

"I know."

She studied my face, apparently in disbelief. "They'll hear," she reasoned.

"I want them to." Tension hardened my neck, shoulders, and arms. My jaw clenched and I could feel my expression pinch with annoyance. My tone was unmistakably sharp when I spoke again. It thundered with a don't-make-me-say-it-twice emphasis as I enunciated each word. "That's. The. Point."

A flush crept across her cheeks, but she obeyed, sitting on the edge of the bed and scooting backwards until she was in the center.

"You're learning, but you need to be taught a lesson. I'm going to fuck you right now. Hard and fast. The floorboards will creak, the headboard will bang against the wall, and you'll scream out with pleasure. I want my father to hear all of it."

Questions welled in Izabelle's eyes, but it wasn't the time to explain, so I let her sit there, leaving all of them unanswered while her chin trembled, and she curled her hands around her middle.

"Can I just ask why you want them to hear? Do you want them to think I'm some kind of whore—some slut with no shame or morals you brought home for a fast fuck? Is it about Marshall's video...?" Her voice trailed off, weak, her breathing rushed, and her chest caving.

"I'm just being the animal you already think I am."

It was fucked-up thing to say, but I had to.

She swallowed and lay back, stiff and fragile-looking. A complete contrast to the sexy curves of her body and her wild curls over the ripples of my down comforter. This was as much to get my point across to her as it was to let my father hear me living out his perverted fantasies. Izabelle wasn't a virgin when I met her, but I'd definitely taken her innocence.

Her chest rose and fell quickly, and my cock tightened as heat revved through me.

"Take off your clothes." I unfastened my pants and tugged them down around my hips, freeing my full length, stroking it while she watched me with worried brown eyes. With my left hand I pulled my shirt over my head, then surveyed her as she toed off her shoes and removed her leggings.

It turned me on to see the way her eyes darted, following my every move. There was a growing hunger in her eyes which wasn't there before. An all-consuming spark glowed in them as she drank in the sight of my cock, then up the tapestry of my tattoos, climbing the dunes of my chest. But, when she locked her gaze on mine, the spark grew into a blazing wildfire as she lifted herself up on her elbows and let her knees hang slightly open.

Hard and ready, I walked up to the edge of the bed. "I want to hear every breath and moan. I can't explain now, but I'm saving you."

She closed her eyes and took a breath, and when she opened them again, the questions were back. *Who are you saving me from?* at the top of the list. In this moment, in light of what I was doing to her, it made it even harder to answer. I hated how it made me feel like the monster I was supposedly protecting her from.

Rather than go down the rabbit hole, I continued stroking myself as I lifted her shirt up around her neck. The swell of her breasts teased me. I leaned down to drag my tongue over each of her pebbled brown nipples, sucking and licking slowly. She muffled a moan, squirming, trembling beneath my lips.

"Let me hear you."

All I got was a nod as Izabelle pulled me flush against her pliant body, pressing her hips up against me. Damn, it was so hard not to bury myself inside her right then and there, but I needed to take the time to do this right if I was going to keep dear old Daddy away from her. I wiggled free from her grasp and continued trailing my tongue down to her flat stomach. I circled her shallow navel, then moved lower until I took the hem of her thin cotton panties between my teeth, tugging down, then licking the warm grooves where the elastic laid.

She arched her back, ruffling her fingers through my hair. Then, an agonized moan slipped from her. "Oh, Xander," she whispered. Her voice was breathy and strained with the same coarse little quiver she made when my fingers were inside her for the first time.

"Louder. I need him to know."

"I want you," she croaked.

I halfway expected my cock to tighten when I heard her response, but it was my heart. It squeezed under the grip of her confession. Izabelle wanted me, craved me as much as I did her. The thought crept under my skin and settled there, igniting me from the inside out. More than a random fuck, it left me with a hunger only she could satisfy.

Suddenly, I needed to feel her, smell her, and taste her sweetness.

Without another word, I slid her panties off and let my tongue graze the soft flesh, the bundle of nerves at the meeting of her thighs. She was clean-shaven and smooth all over. With my fingers, I pried her open, licking and sucking while she writhed, the tension in her legs hard against my arms.

As I quickened my pace, going faster and deeper, I heard the hitch in her voice, and then she released a sharp cry.

"Fuck, yes!" I croaked.

Izabelle bit down hard on her bottom lip, tilting her head back so that her chin was in the air, her throat bared. The delicate column of her neck on display with her breasts peaked to the sky. At her sides, she dug her fingers into the duvet, holding on tight as her back arched and her body trembled.

"Say it," I commanded.

"Fuck me," she yelled, her wild voice echoing off the walls. "Your mouth feels so fucking great. Xander, I need you inside me. Now."

Only when a rush of tremors washed over her did I get to my feet. Seeing her come undone, her golden-brown skin drenched in lamplight, it was hot as hell. A wave of desire surged through me, and I could feel my pulse hammer in my neck. I couldn't resist. I rolled on a condom. My hands steady on her knees, I plunged my cock into her, feeling her wet, hot pussy clench around the thickness. Another wave of shivers as she bucked, riding the orgasm. With it, the headboard banged against the wall and the floorboards creaked as she released another sharp cry.

She felt too good.

I was almost there when I noticed the slow, sexy grin on her distracting mouth. She was ready for another go. I knew if I stayed inside her, I wouldn't be able to hold it much longer, so I pulled out.

"I want to fuck your mouth." I released a low growl.

What I thought would wipe the smile off her face seemed to only widen it. Izabelle didn't hesitate, she sat upright, removed the condom, and glided her lips down the full length of my cock, her slippery, hot mouth sucking and licking. I didn't dare watch her or I'd come, so I dug my fingers into her hair and held her head steady while I pumped myself in and out of her mouth.

"Holy shit." My lungs struggled to keep up with my racing heart. I was boneless and breathless, coming apart as she took me wider and deeper into that filthy mouth of hers. "I'm coming."

I tried to pull out, but she grabbed my ass and tightened her grip, drinking me in.

"Oh, my God. I fucking love you."

CHAPTER FIFTEEN

IZZY

WHEN WE HIT THE BOTTOM OF THE STAIRS, MR. AND MRS. Gale were waiting for us in the parlor doorway.

To say I was mortified would be a gross understatement. I couldn't look at them. I couldn't look at Xander.

Did I like fucking him? Yes. It didn't get better than hate-fucking him so hard. But, did I need his parents tuned in to the surround sound audio? No. A million times no. I only did it for him because I knew deep in my bones that my original suspicion about something awful going on between Xander and is father was basically confirmed.

"Mom." He kissed Evelyn on the cheek, then turned to Mr. Gale. Xander's jawline was hard, distinctive. His stance was noticeably wider, and his chest thrust out. And his tone was rigid. "Father."

Mr. Gale turned his body at an angle instead of facing his son head-on. His eyes were cold, and his mouth pinched. He stiffened. "Xander."

It was the first time I was truly scared. I sensed the challenge between them—Xander's defiance. In that very moment, I realized who I was performing for and why, and I couldn't get out of there fast enough.

"Thank you for inviting me over. Have a great night," I said to his parents without meeting their fixed gazes and rushed out the door.

I was already waiting at the car before Xander made it to the entry. When I looked up, though, the two guys were whispering, but their closed postures and sweeping, sharp gestures made it clear they were arguing. Xander pointed the key fob toward me and pressed the button to unlock the car before turning back to Mr. Gale.

The silent show went on for a few minutes more before Xander stalked away and we sped off. I waited until we rounded the curve into the straightaway before I spoke.

"What would he have done to me?"

He didn't turn to look at me, but I saw his grip tighten around the steering wheel.

"They're all the same. My father, Marshall, Jorden..."

You.

He glanced over as if he could hear my thoughts. "I don't want to be like them."

"Then don't be. Don't hurt me. Be with me," I said.

My heart sank, and I hated it, because I shouldn't have had to beg someone to make that kind of a choice. If it wasn't obvious, what was I doing with him?

What am I doing?

Xander might not have wanted to be like them, but he'd surrounded himself with predators, and it was naive of me to believe he wasn't already cut from the same cloth.

"Xander," I shifted in the seat to face him for the second time in two days. It was time to pry, to find out how much danger I was really in. "What would your father have done to me? Why is he anything like Marshall or Jorden?"

He didn't look at me, but I could almost feel him relenting, the weight of the truth lifting as he unloaded.

"A year ago, Dad left some important papers at home, and Mom asked me to run after him. So I followed him. Only he didn't go to his office. I found him at a seedy-looking motel." He swallowed, and the vein at his temple bulged. "I waited out there for about half an hour before a girl showed up and knocked on his door. She couldn't have been more than fourteen, fifteen, because she was a freshman at Badlands."

"What happened?"

"They were in there for over an hour. He came out first and sped off in his car, but I waited. I had to see her. Fifteen minutes later, she walked out, and I'll never forget the look on her face. She was flushed, and her eyes were red-rimmed, like she'd cried the whole time. The way she was holding her arms over her middle and her body sagged, I knew something had happened, but I didn't want to believe my dad was capable of the things I was imagining. He was my father, the man who I'd looked up to my whole life, and I'd modeled myself in his image. The man who wouldn't allow profanity in his house and fished or played golf with me on weekends. I couldn't make the lines meet."

I pushed my hair out of my face and leaned back against the window while he blinked back tears.

"Go on."

"Anyway, I skipped class and had my friend drop me off at home. Mom is always hopped up on pills and numb to everything, so she didn't even know I was there. I rifled through all his books and papers, and I was just about to give up, tell myself there was a logical reason for what I'd seen. He was on the school board, so maybe the girl was pleading with him for leniency on something, I didn't know. But then the bottom drawer to his desk got stuck when I was pushing it back in.

"There was a false bottom filled with NDAs, voided

checks, and pictures attached. All young girls. The oldest one was sixteen. The worst part was, there were medical records for every one of them, stating the hymen was intact. Fucking virginity tests probably from some asshole doctor friend of his."

"So he thought I was a virgin?"

"Yes." His voice thundered as he released a wicked laugh. "What did you think, he was just a regular pedophile? No, not my father. He wouldn't dare to be run-of-the-mill. The fucking monster loves the hunt. He scouts all over campus. The second you and your father showed up, I knew he'd targeted you. That's why I did what I did in the hallway—why I needed him to hear you today. I had to throw him off your scent."

What the fuck?

Was I supposed to say thanks? Oh, yes. *Thank you so much for proving I was stupid and naive to believe you're actually into me.* I turned to the window and stared out.

There was nothing left to say.

A little more than a half hour later, he dropped me off a few blocks from my dorm in case The Crows or The Ravens were watching, not that they didn't already know we were together after we ran into Jorden and Nic in the hotel. I took the long way up, keeping to the darkest halls and stairs to avoid any run-ins. The whole way, I felt my phone vibrating in my pocket.

I didn't have to look to know it was Xander.

The way we separated, it felt like a point of no return, because how could we go back to pretending, when around every corner there was someone with their sights on me—including Xander? Hotels, motels, young girls, they were all the same. I was heartbroken and empty.

When I made it to my room, I closed the door behind me

and just slid to the floor, the weight of this new world crushing down on me.

"I need you, Dad," I cried.

He couldn't hear me, but I hoped somehow the universe would send him the message. The good thing was, Honoré wasn't around, so I could break down in peace. I scanned the room. My bed seemed like it was still the way I'd left it. My shoes neatly lined up under it. All my movie posters accounted for. I breathed a sigh of relief and got a glimpse at the only silver lining in this oily black haze that was my life.

The cookies on my desk were still unopened.

I peeled myself up off the floor, intent on devouring the whole bag, and that's when I noticed them. Five lipstick tubes lined up on the far-left corner of my desk. Upon closer inspection, next to the tubes, all in a single shade of purple, I found a note written in my roommate's jagged script.

Your perfect shade for the party. You'll want to leave your mark.

Kisses,
Honoré

I swiped them all off the desk and watched them bounce and roll on the threadbare carpet. I thought about calling Xander, but then reminded myself he was one of them. Then I fished my phone out of my pocket. There were three missed messages from him, but I cleared each one and found Dad in my favorites instead.

After the fourth ring, I thought about just hanging up and crying myself to sleep, but then the line clicked, and I heard his familiar, husky voice.

"Izz, I'm so happy you called. I've been having a doozy of a week," his voice bellowed in my ear. "Can you believe I'm homesick already? I miss you so much. I miss your Sunday pancakes and watching Jeopardy with you, but I did find you something purple."

A tear trailed down my cheek as I sat on the bed. I let my weight sink into the mattress as I lifted the tiny horse figurine out of its box. I ran my fingers over the smooth curves, missing Xander in the worst way.

"Yeah?" I swallowed, biting back tears. I couldn't tell him what I was going through. He had real worries that mattered, and I didn't need to add to them. I walked myself into the line of fire, it was going to be up to me to get out.

"So, how's it going?"

"Same," I lied, trying to keep my voice even. Nothing about Wastelands was like where I came from. I'd dealt with regular bullies who put rotten fish in lockers and mean girls with their precious cafeteria seating charts. I'd even had my fair share of run-ins with fights, rec drugs, and bathroom stall bitch fests, but this wasn't that. Bruises healed and paint erased the worst slurs. This was the worst type of violation.

"I love you."

I sniffled and swallowed.

Dad paused briefly, listening, knowing. "You're sure you're okay?"

The door flew open, and of course, in walked Honoré. She did her usual easy stroll into the room and planted herself directly in front of me. Her right arm was folded over her stomach and the elbow of the other arm was propped on it. She rubbed her finger over her top lip.

"Listen, Dad. I'll call you again later. Love you."

"Isn't that sweet? I wonder if Daddy knows what his slutty little daughter has been up to."

I winced and scooted back on my bed to widen the distance between us. "What do you want?"

"Oh nothing." She turned on her heel, set her bags on her bed, and bent down to pick up the lipstick tubes while she kept talking. "I just wondered if you have enough lipstick. Are you going to woman up, or you going to go crawling into your little dark hole and cry like Emily? Who knows? Maybe you'll do us all a favor and end yourself like your mom did."

"Fuck you, Honoré. You don't know me. You don't know anything about my family." I sprang to my feet and strode over until I was right behind her. She swiveled around and our faces were only inches apart. I let my chin drop as I glared up from under my brow into her green eyes. "And don't say another fucking word about my mother."

She released a deep, guttural laugh. "So there is some fight in you. Good, because I was beginning to think this was going to be boring."

A strange calm washed over me. It was almost like I could feel my backbone growing, my skin thickening. I thought, *how funny. Just when you have nothing to lose, you realize you don't have a fuck to give.*

"What happened to you, Honoré? Did they get you, too? Is that how you became a Raven, spreading your toxic unkindness around?" I tilted my head and inhaled as she registered the truth in my words. "Oh, they did get you. So, where's *your* famous video?"

The smug smile slipped from her perfectly lined lips and she whipped her braid off her shoulder. "Say what you want, but I'm a Raven and you're The Feed, and that makes me better than you. After high school, I'll go on to an amazing law firm and end up wealthy and happy, while you're still crawling around on your knees giving blow jobs and trying to find your place at the bottom."

"Is that before or after every Crow took their turn with you? Did they all run a train on you? Is that it? They took their time passing you around?"

Honoré shoved her shoulder into mine, pushing past me, and opened her closet, where she rummaged, apparently for nothing in particular because she didn't blink. She just stood there unseeing, probably wading through some memory while she ran her hands over the fabrics.

Screw her and her head games.

I left and made my way to the common room down the hall. It was mostly empty, except for one girl sitting by the fireplace next to the lounge chairs. She was thin, with bright orangish-red hair and porcelain skin over regal bone structure. I flashed her a quick smile as I passed, but my eyes snagged on the name written on her binder.

Clementine O.

My heart stopped. And I must've been staring, because she cleared her throat and waggled her brows as if to say snap out of it.

I did.

Quickly, too, because I knew I needed to get my shit together if I was going to pick her brain about Marshall. "Sorry, I just...you're Clementine Olivier."

"That'd be me." Again, her thin brows danced with awkward amusement. "And you are...?"

I gulped a mouthful of air and slowly released it from my nose before I spoke. "Izzy, Izabelle Water—

"Ah. The new girl. You've been here, what, a week? Already covered a lot of ground with your new frenemies, I see. What have you got planned for next week, bringing down the—"

"Don't take this the wrong way, but you don't seem like Marshall's type."

She nodded absently, her bottom lip protruding as the corners of her mouth tugged downward. "Wow. You really have a way with words. And here I thought it was your winning personality that caught everyone's attention."

"I didn't mean it like that. It's just, you seem...like you wouldn't give him the time of day. Like if The Crows threatened you, you'd call in your minions and say 'off with his head!'"

She laughed at this, because really, even I had no clue what I was saying. I learned fast that when The Crows picked you, there was little choice in the matter. It was more about how much you could endure, and if you'd still be standing when they were done with you.

"Listen," I started again. "What I'm really attempting to do in the most awkward way possible is to ask how you took Marshall down. I know you copied Emily Sutton's original video from his phone, but when I asked Xander, he couldn't tell me what you did with it, or what you were planning to do."

Clementine's eyes darted to the door before she narrowed them on me. She parted her lips like she was weighing the question against the anxious girl in front of her, angling her body away from me. When she spoke, I noticed the flat tone.

"Why are you in here? Did they send you to find me?"

There it was. The same paranoia that had shadowed me for the past week. The distrust. The intent listening, ready to catch the lies. Mostly, the compulsive need to know what side a person was on in order to assign a threat level.

For her sake, I took a step back and shrugged. "There's going to be a feeding and I'm on the menu."

A mixture of relief, pity, and sympathy flushed her cheeks. "Shit."

"I know. Xander and I were trying to figure out how to get me out of it, but now that's not an option..."

Clementine lifted her chin and squinted, studying me. Her legs, crossed at the ankles, bounced with a nervous tick while she leaned back and folded her arms. "That's the second time you mentioned Xander. He got to you, didn't he?"

"No. Well, yes." I shook my head. "I think I've got him all

wrong, though. He's trying not to be like them. I mean he is one of them, but I think he's different."

She sat up and her fingers went to tapping on her computer keys, then she flipped the screen around to me. I immediately recognized the grainy hotel background and Emily's champagne-colored dress. Except I hadn't seen it at this angle. Clementine pressed a button and the volume notches disappeared one by one before she played the video. This time Emily wasn't talking, she was completely deep-throated on some guy on the bed. As she pulled her head back, I saw the lipstick marks climbing the shaft of the guy's cock.

Lipstick party.

Absently, I placed my hand over my mouth and gasped. I was sick to my stomach.

Clementine tossed me a look, but I couldn't read her expression. Then she pinched her thumb and forefinger together on the trackpad and spread them apart until the screen zoomed in on the guy to whom Emily's mouth was still attached. I thought my heart might beat out of my chest. Xander.

What the...?

"Right about now I assume the words 'what the fuck' are going through your head," Clementine said. "I showed you this video because last year I was you. They don't share the videos unless you disobey them, but if you're all hugged up with Xander, that makes you a target for Marshall. Those two are basically at war. He's going to do everything in his power to take you from Xander. I don't know how you plan to get out of the feeding, but you need to keep your distance from Xander Gale. He's a Crow, and Crows cannot be trusted."

My phone vibrated against my leg and I fished it out of my pocket. It was him. For a moment, I stared at the red and green icons like a fork in the road. No matter how much I thought I liked Xander, I couldn't be with him. I ignored the call and met Clementine's gaze instead.

"Thanks. I needed to see it."

If a feeding was what they wanted, that's exactly what I would give them.

CHAPTER SIXTEEN

XANDER

FRIDAY I AWOKE TO THE SOUND OF MY PHONE VIBRATING across the nightstand. I hoped it was Izabelle, since we hadn't spoken since I dropped her off Sunday. She'd been ignoring my calls and texts, and somehow she'd also managed not to run into me on campus. In the muted sunlight of the morning, I grabbed it and squinted at the bright screen.

Mom: Happy birthday, honey. Where did the years go? I can't believe my baby is already eighteen. Have fun with your friends tonight. Don't worry about your father, we still want to see you tomorrow. Love you.

I rolled out of bed and scrubbed my hand over my face as a message dropped from the top of the screen.

Marshall: Rise and shine birthday boy. Looking forward to your party tonight. Don't even think about backing down. Remember, I've got a video of your little Valentine one way or the other, so it's completely up to you which one we use.

"Fuuuuuck." I could give a shit about the party, but it was Valentine's Day, and I wanted to find a way to make Izabelle understand that I wasn't like Marshall or my father, and right now the best way to prove it seemed to be getting her out of the feeding tonight.

"What's up? You okay?"

I turned to find a shiny black shock of hair sticking out from a mass of blankets. My roommate, Ichiro was staring at me, shielding one eye from the sun. I sighed and blew out a chest full of air.

"Nah, I'm good. I just want this day to be over, that's all."

Ichiro groaned, his voice thick with sleep. "It hasn't even started yet." He pulled the covers back over his head. "By the way, happy birthday."

The rest of the day, as people who I called friends and people who I didn't know all wished me a happy birthday, I resisted the urge to ask them what was so happy about today. Being a legal adult didn't diminish the fact that my father is a fucked-up pedophile and my so-called friend Marshall is a sadistic bully. None of which would convince Izabelle to give me another chance.

As I walked the hall headed for Humanities class, I thought about charging Marshall's dorm and beating him to oblivion, but how did that make me different?

I needed to show Izabelle how much she meant to me. Flowers and chocolates crossed my mind and kept going. How do you show a woman you've only known a dozen days how much she means to you? I needed to get creative, and I only had a few hours to do it.

That's when I passed the art room and an idea hit me. I leaned against the doorframe and cleared my throat. "Mr. Ackerman, do you still have any of that colored paper? I was hoping to snag a dozen or so off of you."

"Absolutely. I have to tell you, Xander, I'm glad to see you embracing your creative side." He walked over to a credenza topped with an array of supplies and pulled a small stack off the top. "Here you go. I hope you'll bring whatever it is you're making to class when you're finished."

I nodded my thanks and left, pulling out the purple sheets. I had two weeks' worth of letters to write.

BY THE TIME I ARRIVED AT THE COUNTRY CLUB THAT night, I'd drained my heart out on paper. What was left flowing through my veins was something like disgust and rage. A deadly mix. I was on a mission to confront Marshall and put a stop to the feedings.

As soon as I opened the door to the Estrada Suite, the blaring music and the chatter of the crowd hit me like a tidal wave. Sudden and breathtaking.

All my senses were overwhelmed. I was spinning out of control. It was a blur of red and pink with hearts everywhere. About fifty sets of eyes were on me. I could smell the antici- pation in the air as I weaved through the foyer and into the living room. The stares, the hushed whispers, every turn of a head, they all left my body pulsing with the mounting pressure.

I wanted to leave, but my heart wouldn't let me. I wasn't about to pick now to start bowing down to Marshall. Not when Izabelle needed me most.

"I can't wait for the show," someone said. I flinched and jerked toward the voice.

Then a girl in the back chimed in. "It's going to be epic."

That's when the cheers and chants began. Louder. Faster. More aggressive with every step I took toward the back where the master suite was. My eyes darted to all the old standbys lining the counters. There were buffets of pills and alcohol. For the guest of honor, a clear glass mixing bowl filled to the top with lipstick tubes in every shade.

I'd seen it all before, but nothing could have prepared me for what was waiting behind the bedroom door.

I knocked with my left hand and turned the handle with my right.

A digital camera was set on a tripod aimed at a king-sized bed. Black satin sheets were draped over the length. And in the middle of it sat my Izabelle in a short purple dress—for easier access.

My heart dropped into my stomach, and I couldn't breathe.

What are you doing?

I didn't have a clue where her head was, but whatever she was up to, she couldn't know how far Marshall would go to prove he was the king of The Crows.

A movement in my periphery snagged my attention. I whipped my head around to find Marshall looking pleased with himself for orchestrating the show, and I marched over to him, fuming, unsure what exactly I was about to do. He didn't even flinch as I stopped within an inch of his face.

"What the fuck are you doing?"

"Showing your girlfriend a good time." He lifted his chin, baring his thick neck, ready for whatever I threw at him.

I wasn't thinking clearly. My head was fuzzy, and every muscle in my body tensed and trembled as I balled my fists, drew my head back, and spit in his face. "Fuck you."

Marshall blinked and flashed a small smile that didn't reach his eyes. He was enjoying this shit, and it pissed me off even more when I didn't get the reaction I was hoping for.

Slowly, he pulled a purple bandanna out of his pocket, flaunting Izabelle's favorite color while he dabbed his cheek. His voice was low and even when he addressed me. "I'm going to let that one slide because I know you got caught up in the game," he said simply, warning vibrating in his husky tone.

I couldn't take it. Fire blazed through me. I turned on my heel, took wide strides over to Izabelle, and led her by the hand to the door. But before we made it out, she tugged on my hand to stop me, and I jerked around.

"What? Are you okay?"

Her smile was somber and pained as she swallowed. She dropped my hand and lowered her chin. "They're never going to leave me alone, and he has the video."

"We have to try." I hated the desperation in my shaky voice. I sounded as weak as I felt.

"It'll just be another day, another hotel room, hallway, dorm...I can't live in fear anymore, and I'm not going to let them run me out of here—"

"She's smart. I can see why you picked this one, Gale," Marshall cut her off, reveling in my dilemma.

Izabelle leaned in close to my ear. "He made me a deal. He said it only has to be you. They just want to watch."

I shook my head, because a deal with Marshall was a deal with the devil himself.

"You can't trust him." Again, my voice wavered. "Please. Let's just go."

I was begging her, and she refused to listen.

She took a step back and fixed me with her pleading eyes. "I have to try," she said, then turned and walked away.

CHAPTER SEVENTEEN

IZZY

"WHERE DO YOU WANT ME?" I ASKED, PRAYING MARSHALL would keep his word. I was standing in the middle of the bedroom, and out of the dozens of eyes on me, I could only focus on the heat and the weight of Xander's stare on my back. But at this particular moment I couldn't trust anyone in the room.

As soon as I arrived at the suite Marshall had whisked me off through the sidelines of cheering people and into the bedroom, where he promptly closed and locked the door. I stood there with the wall's cold wood holding me upright, shaking, and wondering how hard the fall would be if I jumped out the window. If one teensy thing didn't go according to my plan, it would mean my ruin.

Snapping to, I flitted a glance over my shoulder at Xander that I meant to be reassuring, but the way his shoulders slumped, I knew I misfired.

So be it.

"Let's call in the viewers first," Marshall announced.

I nodded and remained at the center of the room, careful to keep my back to the camera while the unnamed faces of

Wastelands' hallways filed into the empty spaces, into chairs, on the floor, against the walls.

"All right. Thanks, everyone, for coming. The feeding will commence shortly, but I need to take care of a few quick orders of business. One, I want to make sure everyone checked their phones at the door. You know the rules. We'll make sure you all have a link in the event our star decides to snitch." A hum of yesses and nods wafted over the crowd. "Okay, then. I just want to say Happy Valentine's Day for all you lovebirds. You demanded, and, as your trusted *king*, and a man of my word, I have supplied."

I wanted to gag at the way he rubbed his hands together with that seedy look in his eyes.

"We've got a special treat for you tonight. On his birthday, one of our very own, Xander Gale, will be gifting us with a show I know will live up to the hype. And joining him, the newest member of The Feed—Izzy!"

This guy is off his fucking rocker.

Again, the cheers and applause ramped up and died down, quickly replaced by the buzz of anticipation. I felt like I was in the middle of *The Hunger Games,* with all the palpable excitement, the thrill of witnessing a person be destroyed.

"Xander." Marshall sliced the air with his hand, gesturing to the bed, and Jorden Battle, who was on camera duty, panned the room. I turned my back while Xander walked forward painstakingly slowly, then plopped down on the mattress with a small bounce.

"Maybe we can give him some encouragement, guys," Marshall added.

At his sides were the Harding twins and Honoré standing guard.

"Although we'd love to see how Izzy does it." He laughed and lifted his chin quickly, holding up a finger as if something just occurred to him. "Oh, just to cover my bases... We don't need any further incidents. We don't do force. For the camera, I need you to state your agreement to the sexual acts in which you are about to partake?"

I thought about what he said earlier, when it was just the two of us in this room.

Insurance is so important.

He'd patted the breast pocket of his blazer where he'd stashed his phone and immediately my mind went to the video of me and Xander. It was clear enough, and the angle just so, to make out my face and Xander's cock plunging into me. I was in complete survival mode and left with no choice but to do the unthinkable if my plan was going to work.

I searched into the crowd and spotted Abbie in place by the door, so she could break away easily. Owen was by the window. When I met his stony gaze, he nodded, which meant he'd gotten his phone into the room. That was the signal. He was ready, and Clementine was waiting.

I can't believe I'm going to fucking do this.

A wave of heat washed over me, I could barely breathe, and for a split second I thought my legs would give out. Between the ringing in my ears and my chest caving in, I could very well have been about to faint or have a heart attack, but I pushed it all away. I was light-headed at the thought of what I was about to do, but I turned on my tunnel vision. Falling apart now wasn't an option.

Marshall cleared his throat and I glanced back at him.

Here goes nothing.

"Yes." My voice was choked with tears.

"Well then, let's get started."

I took the few steps to the bed where Xander was sitting on the edge, his face pale. He looked up at me from under heavy brows. His eyes were an overcast blue and filled with apologies. I kneeled, peeling my dress straps off my shoulders and letting my dress pool to the floor. I was completely nude.

The crowd hummed their approval.

Absently, I scratched an itch at the corner of my mouth, and as I looked at the deep purple stain on my hand, I realized I'd forgotten all about the lipstick.

"You don't have to do this," Xander whispered.

"We haven't got all night. Can we go a little faster?" Marshall scoffed with traces of annoyance and smugness.

He wasn't the only one who wanted to hurry and get this over with.

"Sit back," I said to Xander, who hesitantly obliged. As he did, I unbuckled his belt and unzipped his pants, freeing the full length of his already-hardened cock. He flushed, as if embarrassed by the evidence that he was turned on.

How can you be mortified when **I'm** *the one on my knees, about to surrender the last of my innocence?*

I was right there with him, though, my heart racing, the beat pounding in my ears. Shame didn't even cover what I was feeling at the pull low and tight in my belly. How could I be turned on when I was being sacrificed? Between my thighs, I could feel myself getting wet as I stroked him. Gently at first, then I quickened the pace before taking him into my watering mouth.

"Fuck that's hot," a guy said, reminding me we weren't alone.

Even though we had an audience, I blocked them out and it was just us two. I alternated between fast and slow. Licking and sucking around the veiny thickness, I drank in his bitter sweetness. Xander shifted, his body tensing, cock throbbing against my tongue. He rocked, slippery and wet, down my throat, fucking my mouth hard and deep. He didn't grab my hair the way he'd done in the hotel, but I could tell he wanted to as he pulled his bottom lip between his teeth and bit down hard enough to nearly break skin.

I was completely aroused.

Down his shaft, I played with the purple rainbow fading up to the tip.

This was what they wanted, a fucking show. But if I was going to go down for the sake of entertainment, I was damn well going to treat them to a show they'd never seen before.

Just when Xander stiffened in my mouth, I pulled my head back, got to my feet, and climbed on top of him.

"Holy shit. She's going to fuck him right here." The crowd buzzed and the volume in the room rose, but I wasn't going to stop.

My knees slid over the black satin sheets as I straddled him, centered him at the meeting between my thighs, and forced him inside my blazing hot flesh until I was full. I lifted and slammed down again and again as Xander grabbed my ass and spread me wider to accept all of him.

"Fuck," he said on a shallow breath. "Why are you doing this here?"

"This is what they want. They want to humiliate me. But trust me, I'm not playing by their rules."

It was like a lightbulb went off in him. His expression brightened, and he opened his half-lidded eyes wide to meet my gaze. We were speaking without saying a word. Maybe I *could* trust him.

Just you and me.

I felt like I might burst as he lifted his hips and I crashed down onto him harder and faster. Then, amazingly, I came apart, collapsing onto him as he pumped and shivered beneath me. My skin pulsed and blazed everywhere it touched his, and he was holding me so tight I almost forgot where we were.

"Talk about enthusiasm..." Marshall went back to his emcee duties. "I don't know about you, but I can't wait to see what she does next."

Next?

My heartbeat sped up again as I lifted my head and turned to meet his gaze. He was smarmy and underhanded, and I knew he had something up his sleeve.

In fact, I was counting on it.

While Marshall walked to the center of the room to address his willfully blind followers, I turned to face the door, searching the faces until I found Abbie's red frames and bright amber eyes waiting for my signal.

I nodded and she was gone.

Please let this work.

Lifting off of Xander, I pulled my dress on and slipped the straps back up over my shoulders before turning to Marshall. As expected, behind him were the Harding Twins, flanking Honoré's shoulders. She was hanging on his every word—right where I needed her to be.

Three, two, one.

"What do you say? Did I live up to the hype? Did you guys enjoy the show?" I asked, and all eyes were on me, including a searing pair attached to Marshall. Even though I wanted to tuck myself away in a dark hole and never come out, this wasn't over. The crowd response was raucous and wild. I took it as a resounding yes.

"What are—"

"It turns out that Marshall, your fearless leader, has another surprise for you. He's brimming with special treats tonight." I was talking fast, leaving no room for anyone to get a word in edgewise. My game face was firmly in place.

"For his best friend's birthday, he's going to give you guys an encore presentation. Joining him will be your queen Raven and my favorite roommate, Honoré Montgomery."

Gasps pinballed off the walls, and I led the applause.

Wide-eyed terror flashed in Marshall and Honoré's eyes. She looked like her knees might buckle. He rocked back and forth, shifting from one foot to the other, his chest puffed out. It didn't seem as if they liked the taste of their own medicine.

"Come on, guys, you can do better than that. Let them really hear how much you want to see what they'll do next."

The room echoed with whistles and shouts, people clapping, stomping, and rooting them on.

"You can do this."

"Fuck, yeah. I'm so glad I came tonight."

Another. "I've been dying to see you guys together. I knew they were a thing."

Far off in the back, I heard two girls talking. "This beats hearts and chocolate any day."

Yes, it did.

"Guys." I whirled around, clapping my hands. "Wait a minute. You know the rules. We don't do force." I turned to the deceitful duo. "Do you guys agree to the sexual acts in which you're about to partake?"

A small bit of joy filtered the venom coursing through my veins as Honoré froze and pressed a hand to her heart. Her lips quivered, and tears welled in her glossy green eyes. As expected, they both consented, and while they began stripping off their clothes, I peeked over to find Owen recording, which meant he'd already texted Clementine. While she was in Marshall's cloud deleting the Creekside video of me and Xander from all Marshall's devices, I eased my way over to Jorden and the camera on the tripod.

Once Honoré's throat was full, I began my mental countdown.

Within seconds, the fire alarm blared through the room.

I stood completely still as chaos ensued.

While some funneled through the single door, others darted every which way, trying to decide whether it was a real emergency. But I knew different.

I knew that, like Owen and Clementine, Abbie did her part, and now it was my turn.

The moment Jorden turned away I fiddled with the camera, deleted the video, and disappeared into the crowd, leaving my undoing and Xander behind.

By the time I made it to the stables, I was physically and emotionally drained. Embarrassment seized me. My throat thickened with sobs while sorrow shredded my insides. My scalp prickled with shame, the guilt over what I'd done tormenting me. It took root in my heart, weighing me down, drowning me in humiliation. I didn't know what I was going to say when I faced them around campus. I wanted to disappear—to curl up and die on the spot, but that would mean they'd won.

My phone pinged and my screen glowed with a group message.

Marshall: You just bought yourself a world of trouble.

Honoré: This isn't over. If I have to spend the rest of my life trying, I'm going to make you suffer for what you've done.

Jorden: The game is over. This is war.

Penny: You can run... You know the rest.

Izabelle: "Insurance is so important." Check your cloud.

Along with my videos, turned out Marshall had a whole deck full of tricks, and now they were all in my hands. Tears trailed down my cheeks as I lifted my chin. One thing was for sure. I might now be an empty shell of who I was, but they didn't take me down. They'd sought me out and tried to ruin me socially and sexually, fully intending to throw me out like trash, but I was still here.

Xander or no Xander, The Crows would have to find someone else to feed on.

But that was just it. I couldn't let this happen to anyone else.

CHAPTER EIGHTEEN

XANDER

GRAVEL CRUNCHED UNDER MY FEET AS I WALKED SLOWLY toward Izabelle at the far end of the stable.

She sighed and deflated as soon as she seemed to realize it was me.

"How did you find me?" She slumped against the wall, all her earlier bravado gone. She wasn't the fragile girl I met at my parents' house, either. In fact, everything about her was different. Wilted and watered down.

From the way her arms hung at her sides but her chin remained lifted, I could tell she'd learned the hard lesson: victory in war wasn't for the faint of heart.

"You know they're never going to give up. What you did, it's just the beginning."

With every step I took, the light grew stronger on her face. The gravity of what she'd been through was etched somewhere between the lines and the tears swimming in her eyes. Her knitted brows and smeared lipstick were proof that she was harder somehow.

"I'm counting on it." She gritted her teeth.

"Yeah?"

"Why are you here, Xander?" She blinked up at me. Anger flashed in her eyes before she closed them and bowed her head. "Shouldn't you be with your murder of Crows and the unkindness of Ravens, plotting your revenge on me? The rest of them are." Her voice croaked, thick with emotion, and my pulse quickened as she lifted her phone in the air, shaking it.

I knew they wouldn't waste any time gunning for her. It was the second most important reason I was here, the first being the unyielding urgency to tell Izabelle how I felt about her. As I crouched down and sat beside her, our shoulders touching, I finally breathed.

"I'm not like them anymore. I'm done being a Crow."

I felt her shoulders tense, and I expected her to recoil, but Izabelle surprised me by leaning closer and crossing her ankles in front of her.

"I know." She gave a mirthless laugh as she wrapped a curl around her finger. "Do you ever feel like you can take on the world for someone else and keep you head, but when it comes to you, after a certain point, you're just, like, fed up?" She shrugged. "That's where I am at right now. I'm sick and tired of everyone in this wasteland putting their hand out for a piece of me—"

"I love you."

My voice was only a whisper, but from her small gasp, I knew she hadn't been expecting me to say it. Not like this. While we were having sex, sure. It could be explained away as lust in the moment. But this was flat-out real, surrounded by nothing to detract from it. Even though I'd been feeling it creep into my heart, I still hadn't expected to say it—to mean it.

Her expression softened, but her shoulders stiffened, like she wasn't exactly sure what to do with my confession.

"I wanted to cancel the party and just have a nice night with you. I wanted to buy you something to show you how

I'm feeling, but I didn't want you to think I was trying to buy you, so..." I jammed my hand in my coat pocket and pulled out the purple envelopes.

"What are those?"

"This is me trying to earn your heart." I handed her the numbered letters. "There's twelve in all. One for every day I've known you."

Tears shimmered in her eyes as she sat them on her legs and began opening the first one. I tilted my head to read along.

The first day I met you, Izabelle Waters, you asked me if you'd done something wrong when I stopped kissing you. It took me all this time to realize that I stopped because I was consumed by you. Deep down. I knew I wanted you then, I just didn't understand how much I needed you...

Izabelle peeked up at me, sheepish and coy, as a small grin toyed at her mouth. After a few seconds, though, she finished reading the letter and moved on to the next, and the next, until she made her way through the full dozen. Then she slid her right hand over to mine and twined our fingers together.

"I'm thinking we'll call it...taming of the Crow." She giggled, and I loved the way she looked like she was glowing from the inside. There was a fire inside her that blazed brightest for me.

Warmth filled my heart. I was weightless, my spirits soaring as I tipped her chin up and brushed my lips over hers. "You're real funny." I grinned against her mouth. Suddenly, we were both laughing too hard, smiling too hard, despite the darkness closing in on us.

At Izabelle's side, the horses began to squeal and snort.

"Shut up Jigsaw," we both yelled.

I kissed her harder, smiling the whole time, reveling in the moment. I knew I'd never get enough of this brown-eyed girl who devastated a wasteland, but if she thought this was a happy ending... If that's what she was telling herself now, I knew better. I knew beyond a shadow of a doubt that she'd hate what was waiting for us around the corner.

But maybe, just maybe, together we were enough to over-come murder and unkindness.

"What's the plan?" I asked.

"I'm going to take Marshall down."

We weren't done yet.

Not by a long shot.

The End

Enjoyed this story? Be sure to leave a **review**! Book two in this series is coming soon!

ALSO BY MIA HEINTZELMAN

THE ALL MIXED UP SERIES

(Each book can be read as a standalone)

Mixed Signals

Mixed Match

Mixed Emotions

STANDALONES

It's Got A Ring To It - Summer 2020

The Stack w/a Emmaline Zanthi

Wrapped up in beau

ABOUT THE AUTHOR

Mia Heintzelman is a graduate of the University of California, Berkeley and the University of Nevada, Las Vegas. An avid reader, she always has a book in her purse, loves to pair sweet and spicy tea with fluffy socks, and can't go wrong with polka dots and pearls. She lives in Las Vegas with her husband and two children.

Want to hang out with the author, win book prizes, see the cool covers first, receive alerts about Advanced Reader Copies (ARCs), and support Margo's books on social media? Join MIAMORS, Mia's street team and reader group on Facebook!

You can also sign up for On the Dot, Mia's newsletter here.
http://www.miaheintzelman.com/newsletter.html

facebook.com/miaheintzelmanauthor

twitter.com/miaheintzelman

instagram.com/miaheintzelmanauthor

bookbub.com/profile/mia-l-heintzelman

www.ingramcontent.com/pod-product-compliance
Lightning Source LLC
Chambersburg PA
CBHW020247150626
46552CB00020B/646